口說
職場生活英文片語會話

◎ 王仁癸 著 ◎

書泉出版社 印行

本書內容以實用為導向，以片語為主軸，來展開場景式的對話，同時將一些相關的片語集中在一起，有助於讀者了解在哪種場景下會出現哪些片語，以及熟習口說的詞彙、句型與回答技巧，對於想提升職場英文能力的上班族，幫助甚大。

本書專為職場的新鮮人或是上班族精心撰寫的，其特點為：

1. 本書的分類為三大單元，第一單元為職場工作場景片語，第二單元為職場生活場景片語，第三單元為職場旅遊場景片語。

2. 本書片語會話例句強調口說節奏感，以職場溝通實用為導向。

3. 本書以對話方式來呈現片語，其目的是要學習口說片語與對話技巧，能讓讀者覺得生動有趣。

4. 目前市面上的片語書籍例句，都是用學術性語言編寫，造成讀者在口說語言的單字與句型都不善於使用；而本書以職場生活場景來編排，能方便讀者理解和記憶。

最後，熟習本書內容，將有助於TOEIC考試，同時也有助於提升上班族的英文能力與提高職場的升遷機會，更有機會讓你成為國際商務人才。

王仁癸

PART 目錄 _Contents_

第 **1** 單元 **職場工作場景片語** ▶▶ 001

- 🔵 1-01 **01** 介紹 /002
- 🔵 1-02 **02** 人才招募 /017
- 🔵 1-03 **03** 工作溝通 /036
- 🔵 1-04 **04** 工作表現 /080
- 🔵 1-05 **05** 公司 /104

第 **2** 單元 **職場生活場景片語** ▶▶ 171

- 🔵 2-01 **01** 人際關係 /172
- 🔵 2-02 **02** 金錢場景 /193
- 🔵 2-03 **03** 健康場景 /212
- 🔵 2-04 **04** 情緒場景 /232
- 🔵 2-05 **05** 時間場景 /254
- 🔵 2-06 **06** 購物消費 /267

第 **3** 單元 **職場旅遊場景片語** ▶▶ 277

- 🔵 3-01 **01** 機場 /278
- 🔵 3-02 **02** 餐廳 /290
- 🔵 3-03 **03** 出差飯店住宿 /301
- 🔵 3-04 **04** 放輕鬆 /310
- 🔵 3-05 **05** 興趣 /322

第 **1** 單元

職場工作場景片語

01 介紹
（社交場景、問候、道別、找路）

02 人才招募
（履歷表、面試、教育訓練）

03 工作溝通
（電話、會議、產品）

04 工作表現
（工作情況、工作忙、行銷）

05 公司
（公務處理、員工、辦公室瑣事、公司、科技）

01 介紹

(一) 社交場景

▶▶ business card 名片

A : I'm Vivian. This is my business card.

B : Thank you. Here is mine.

A : 我是薇薇安,這是我的名片。

B : 謝謝,這是我的。

▶▶ go by 又稱

A : It was so nice meeting you. What did you say your name was?

B : My name is David, but I also go by Dave.

A : 很高興見到你,你說你的名字是什麼?

B : 我的名字叫大衛,但是我也叫戴夫。

▶▶ in charge of 負責

A: This is Mary. She is in charge of the accounting department.

B: Nice to meet you.

> **A**: 這位是瑪麗，她是負責會計部門。
>
> **B**: 很高興見到你。

Nice to meet you. = Pleased to meet you. = Glad to meet you. (這些句中的 meet，可用 see 代替 meet。)

▶▶ look after 負責

指工作上的打理或處理，look after = be in charge of；當 look after 當「負責」的意義時，look after ＋工作相關名稱，如 She looks after our company's finances. (她負責我們公司的財務。)，look after 也有「照顧」的意思，Who is loving looking after the children? (誰喜歡照顧小孩呢？)

A: I'd like to introduce you to Mr. Lee. He looks after our sales department.

B: It's great.

：我想介紹你認識李先生，他負責我們的銷售部門。

B ：太棒了。

▶▶ make sb.'s acquaintance 認識

解說
用在初次相識的情境下。

A ：It's a pleasure to make your acquaintance.

B ：Me, too.

A ：很高興認識你。

B ：我也是。

▶▶ on behalf of 代表

A ：On behalf of my company, I am very glad to welcome you here.

B ：It's a pleasure to see you here, too.

：我代表我的公司，很高興在這裡歡迎你。

：我也很高興在這裡見到你。

補充

I'm representing my company.（我代表我的公司。）

▶▶ set sb. up 介紹某人給

解說

用在介紹異性；若用 introduce（介紹）這個單字，為商業場合中的正式用法，為在促使雙方互相認識。

：I am going out with Kim tonight.

：Do you think you can set me up with one of your friends?

：我今晚要跟金出去。

：你可以介紹你的朋友給我嗎？

1. set sb. up = fix sb. up = hook sb. up
2. go out with + sb. 指跟異性交往出去玩。

▶▶ welcome to 歡迎光臨

此片語後面要接地點。

A : Welcome to Asus company. It's nice to meet you.

B : Nice to see you, too.

A : 歡迎來到華碩公司,很高興見到你。

B : 我也很高興見到你。

(二) 問候

▶▶ a million dollars 很棒／好極了

A : How are you doing?

B : I feel like a million dollars.

A : 你好嗎?

B : 我覺得好極了啊。

1. I feel like a million dollars. 中文直譯為「我感覺像一百萬美元」，引申為我中了一百萬美元，心情是那麼棒，而這裡的 dollar 也可以用 buck（美金一元）來代替。
2. How are you doing?（你好嗎？），用在熟識朋友間；How are you?（你好嗎？），用在正式場合中。
3. 其他問候句有 How are you getting along?（你好嗎？）；How have you been?（你最近好嗎？）；How's it going?（近況如何？）；What's up?（近況如何？），此句常用在年輕人之間的對話。

▶▶ be pleased to 很高興

A'：I'm pleased to meet you.

B'：I'm happy to meet you, too.

A'：我很高興見到你。

B'：我也很高興見到你。

be pleased to = be happy to

PART

▶▶ couldn't be better 很棒／好極了

 : How have you been recently?

B : It couldn't be better.

> **A** ：近況如何？
> **B** ：好極了。

補充

很棒的英文其他說法有 fantastic ／ excellent ／ wonderful ／ in-credible ／ great。

▶▶ couldn't be worse 很糟糕

 : How is everything going?

B : It couldn't be worse.

> **A** ：一切還好嗎？
> **B** ：糟糕透頂了。

補充

很糟糕的英文其他說法有 terrific ／ worse。

▶▶ same old 老樣子

A: How is your company doing these days?

B: Same old.

A: 最近你們公司經營怎麼樣呢？

B: 老樣子。

補充

1. 句型應用：how is + 人？（某人你好嗎？）；how is + 物？（某物如何呢？），比如 How is your work?（你的工作如何呢？）、How is your company?（你的公司營運如何？）

2. 強調沒有改變，可用這些句型代替 Same old.（老樣子。）So so.（馬馬虎虎。）The same as usual.（還是這樣。）I don't care.（我不在乎。）Nothing has changed.（什麼都沒變。）I can't complain.（還可以。）It doesn't make any difference.（沒什麼差別。）It's all same to me.（對我都沒差。）Both are good with me.（兩個對我都一樣。）

(三) 道別

▶▶ # Have a blessed day
願你有很受祝福的一天

: Have a blessed day.

B: You, too.

> : 願你有很受祝福的一天。
>
> **B**: 你也一樣。

補充

1. 此類似片語為 Have a good day.（祝你有美好的一天。）Have a good night.（祝你有美好的夜晚。）Have a good weekend.（祝你有美好的週末。）Have a nice trip.（祝你旅途愉快。）
2. You, too. = Same to you.

▶▶ # Have a good day 祝你有美好的一天

解說

社交情境中分開的道別語。

: Wait a moment. I have to go back to the office.

B: Have a good day.

：等一下，我必須回辦公室。

：祝你有美好的一天。

(補)(充)

1. Have a good day. = Have a nice day. = Have a great day. = Have a wonderful day.
2. Wait a moment. = Just a minute.（等一下）；go back to（回到）

▶▶ **hear from** 收到…的來信

(解)(說)

指收到某人的來信或聽到某人的訊息。

：Let's meet again sometime.

：I'll be waiting to hear from you.

：讓我們改天見面吧。

：我會等你的消息。

(補)(充)

sometime 改天 = some other day 改天 = take a rain check 改天；
wait to 等待。

▶▶ keep in touch 保持聯繫

A: I'm going to New York on business for two months.

B: Let's keep in touch.

A: 我會去紐約出差兩個月。

B: 讓我們保持聯繫吧。

on business = be on a business trip

▶▶ make a move 該走／開始行動

A: It's about time we make a move.

B: Sure. You'd better get going or you will miss the airplane.

A: 我們該走了。

B: 沒錯，你們最好出發，否則你們會趕不上飛機。

PART

捉緊時間常用片語 get going ／ get coming ／ come on。

▶▶ **Nice talking to you.** 和你談話很開心

Ａ：Nice talking to you.

Ｂ：Same here.

Ａ：和你談話很開心。
Ｂ：我也是。

Nice talking to you. = Nice chatting to you.

▶▶ **See you later** 再見

Ａ：I have to go to the company. Good bye.

Ｂ：See you later.

Ａ：我要回公司，再見。
Ｂ：再見。

1. 與人道別常用「再見」的常用語，Good bye. 為正式用法；
   bye 為非正式用法，用在熟識朋友之間的再見。
2. See you later. = Catch you soon. = See you around. = Catch you later.

▶▶ Take care 保重

A' : Time up. I have to go.

B' : Take care. Keep in touch.

A' : 時間到了，我必須要走了。

B' : 要保重，保持聯繫。

time up 時間到了；keep in touch 保持聯繫。

(四) 找路

▶▶ excuse me 對不起

指用在引起別人的注意。

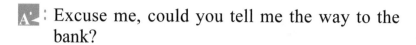

A：Excuse me, could you tell me the way to the bank?

B：Go straight along this street and you'll come to it.

A：對不起，你能告訴我到銀行的路嗎？
B：順著這條路直走，你就會找到。

▶▶ drive straight 直開

A：Drive straight on until you reach the gas station.

B：Thank you.

A：直開你就會到達加油站。
B：謝謝。

▶▶ go straight 直走

A：Can you tell me how to get to the Grand Hotel?

B：Go straight and turn right. You will see the hotel.

Ａ：你能告訴我圓山飯店怎麼走？

Ｂ：直走和右轉，你就會看到飯店。

▶▶ the way to 去…的路

Ａ：Would you show me the way to the post office?

Ｂ：Of course.

Ａ：你能告知我去郵局的路嗎？

Ｂ：沒問題。

補充

找路場景常用句型，I'm completely lost.（我迷路了。）I have no idea where I am.（我不知道我在哪裡。）

02 人才招募

(一) 履歷表

▶▶ apply for 申請

A : You should apply for that job. The pay is reasonable.

B : But I heard the boss is tough.

> **A** : 你應該申請那份工作,待遇很合理。
>
> **B** : 但是我聽說這老闆很嚴苛。

補充

1. 待遇很好表示:The pay is good. = The pay is great. = The pay is fine.
2. 待遇合理表示:The pay is reasonable. = The pay is decent.
3. 待遇差表示:The pay is low. = The pay is poor.

▶▶ attach to 附上

A : Please attach a picture to your résumé if you are interested in this position. And please send your résumé with a picture to my email box.

B : I know résumés without personal photo won't be considered.

如果你對這職位有興趣,請在你的履歷表上附上一張照片,寄到我的電子信箱。

B. 我知道沒有個人相片的履歷表,是不予考慮的。

▶▶ be willing to + V 願意

(解說)

指樂意或情願做某事;而相反詞「不願意」為 be unwilling to + V。

A. Have you got any experience in this field?

B. I'm afraid not, but I'm willing to learn and I'm willing to try.

 你有這領域相關經驗嗎?

B. 很遺憾,沒有,但是我願意學,我願意嘗試。

(補充)

I worked at + 職位(我過去擔任…),比如 I worked at an advertising agency.(我過去擔任廣告代理商。)

▶▶ fill in 填寫

 Don't leave any spaces blank when you fill in the application form.

B : You are right.

A : 當你填寫申請表時，不要留下任何空格。

B : 你說得很對。

補充

fill in = fill out = fill up，一般常用句型為 Please fill in ／ out ／ up this form.（請填寫這個表格。）

▶▶ closing date 截止日期

A : I have to fill out the online job application form to apply for the position. Someone just told me the closing date is tomorrow.

B : If I were you, I'd make it my first priority.

A : 我必須填寫線上工作申請表格來應徵這職位，剛剛有人告訴我，截止日期是明天。

B : 如果我是你，我會讓它成為我的首要任務。（這句話表示消息是正確的）

補充

1. first priority 首要任務／第一優先。
2. make（使／讓）用法：
   (1) make + 受詞 + N make me a model（讓我成為模特兒）
   (2) make + 受詞 + Adj. make me uncomfortable（讓我不舒服）
   (3) make + 受詞 + V make me think（讓我思考）
   (4) make + 受詞 + P.P. make my car fixed（讓我的車被修理了）

▶▶ fill out 填寫

A: To apply for the position, you have to fill out the application form.

B: You're right. I just found today is the due day of application.

A: 要申請這個職位，你一定要填寫申請表格。

B: 沒錯，我剛發現今天是申請的最後一天。

補充

fill out = fill in = complete

▶▶ go over 檢查

A : Remember: Be sure not to make any typo errors in the résumé.

B : OK. I will go over the résumé in detail.

A : 請記住：要確定履歷表上不要有任何打字錯誤。

B : 好的，我會仔細檢查履歷表。

OK. = All right.（好。）

▶▶ in sb.'s opinion 依某人看來

A : There are a few typos in the résumé.

B : In my opinion, it leaves a really bad impression on the interviewer.

A : 履歷表上有一些打字錯誤。

B : 依我看來，那真的會讓面試官留下不好的印象。

補充

面試相關用語 a letter of reference 推薦信、opening ／ vacancy 空缺（職位）、employment contract 工作契約、more room for personal growth 更多個人成長的空間、more challenging 更多挑戰、hold a driver's license 擁有一張駕駛執照、past work experience 過去工作經驗。

▶▶ send in 寄出

解說

指參賽作品或求職信的提交，透過郵寄或呈遞的方式。

 : I formally sent in my résumé today.

 : Now, you just have to wait for them to respond.

 : 我今天正式地寄出了我的履歷表。

 : 現在，你必須等待他們的回覆。

(二) 面試

▶▶ a good look for 很適合

 : What do you think of the applicant?

 : Honestly, I don't think he's a good look for your company.

PART 1

A: 你認為這位求職者怎麼樣？

B: 老實說，我認為他很不適合你的公司。

補充

評價常用句型 What do you think of + N...（你認為…怎麼樣？）
／ How do you like + N...（你認為…如何？）

▶▶ A as well as B A以及B

A: I'd like to know more about your company's benefits.

B: If you successfully pass the 3-month trial period, you will enjoy meal allowances as well as trip abroad.

A: 我想要了解更多有關你們公司的福利。

B: 如果你成功通過3個月的試用期，你會享有員工伙食補助以及員工出國旅遊。

補充

meal allowances 伙食補助；trip abroad 出國旅遊。

023

▶▶ decide on 決定

指考慮後再做決定，等於 make up sb.'s mind。

 What company did you finally decide on?

 I still haven't made up my mind.

 你最後決定去哪間公司呢？

 我還沒做決定。

補充

1. 面試情境常用句型有 Can you sell yourself in three minutes? （你能在 3 分鐘內介紹你自己嗎？）Why did you quit your last job?（你為什麼辭去上一個工作呢？）Why are you leaving your last job?（你為什麼離開上一個工作呢？）Why did you leave your job?（你為什離開你的工作呢？）Why are you looking for a new job?（你為什麼要尋找新工作呢？）What is your strongest trait?（你的最大優點是什麼？）If opportunity knocks, I will take it.（如果機會來臨，我會捉住。）What do you think you are worth?（你認為你的價值是什麼呢？）
2. 面試情境常用句型有 go for it（大膽試一試）、no opportunity for advancement（沒有升遷機會）、benefit from（從…中受益）、job description（工作描述）、narrow-minded（心胸狹窄）、get my points across（了解我的觀點）、easy-going（容易相處的）、a sense of humor（幽默感）、a sense of accomplishment（成就感）。

PART

▶▶ dog-eat-dog world 競爭激烈的世界

直譯爲「狗吃狗的世界」，是在弱肉強食的世界中才會發生，
一般引申爲「自相殘殺的世界」或「競爭激烈的世界」，等於
competitive world（競爭激烈的世界）。

A： I was told that there are over 200 applicants for the position.

B： Well, it's a dog-eat-dog world out there, and you have to try your best to get the position.

A： 我聽說有超過200人申請這個職位。

B： 嗯，外面世界競爭激烈，而你必須盡最大努力來得到這個職位。

▶▶ education background 教育背景

A： What is your education background?

B： I went to undergraduate in Tunghai University, with the major of management.

A： 你的教育背景是什麼呢？

B： 我東海大學畢業，主修管理。

▶▶ first impression 第一印象

A : There is only one chance to make a first impression.

B : So, you never get a second chance to make a first impression.

A : 給別人第一印象，只有一次機會。
B : 所以，你不會有第二次機會給人第一印象。

▶▶ graduate from 從…畢業

A : Which university did you graduate from?

B : I graduated from Taiwan University.

A : 你哪一間學校畢業呢？
B : 我畢業於臺灣大學。

▶▶ in the field 在該領域

A : Do you have any experience in this area?

B : I'm afraid not. Though I have no experience in the field, I'm willing to learn.

: 你有該領域的任何經驗嗎？

: 恐怕沒有，雖然我沒有該領域的工作經驗，但是我願意學。

補充

in the field = in the area

▶▶ **measure up** 符合

解說

指符合標準或達到期望。

: I heard you interviewed with the company. How did it go?

: The boss set high standards. I feel that I didn't measure up to what he is looking for.

: 我聽說你到這家公司面試，結果怎麼樣呢？

: 這老闆設定了很高的標準，我覺得我不符合他的需要。

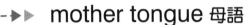

PART

1

▶▶ mother tongue 母語

A : How many languages do you speak?

B : Two. Besides Chinese, my mother tongue, I can also speak English.

A : 你會說幾種語言呢？

B : 兩種，除了我的母語中文外，我還會說英語。

補充

mother tongue = first language = native language

▶▶ the three month trial 3個月試用期

A : Do you think I will pass the three month trial?

B : Yes, I think so, because you learn more and have a better attitude.

A : 你認為我會通過3個月試用期嗎？

B : 我認為可以，因為你學得多和態度佳。

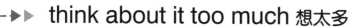

▶▶ think about it too much 想太多

A : I'm so worried about today's interview.

B : Try not to think about it too much.

A : 我很擔心今天的面試。

B : 盡量不要想太多。

面試的心態 Be clear, be confident, be proactive.（要明確，要有信心，要主動積極。）

▶▶ well-qualified 合格

A : The company is looking for a well-qualified and experienced accountant.

B : I am sure you can get the job if you try.

A : 這家公司正在尋找一位合格與有經驗的會計。

B : 如果你去應徵的話，我相信你會得到這份工作。

PART

▶▶ work as 擔任

A : Have you got any experience in finance?

B : I worked as an accountant in a small and medium enterprise for three years.

A : 你有任何財務的工作經驗嗎？
B : 我在一家中小企業擔任會計3年。

work as = serve as；work for（為…而工作）

(三) 教育訓練

▶▶ a crash course 速成班

A : Before taking office, I will need to give you a crash course in finances.

B : I am so excited; I can hardly wait.

A : 在就職前，我要給你上財務速成班。
B : 我超興奮的，我等不及了。

▶▶ be filled up to capacity 客滿

be filled up capacity 也等於 be closed，比如 The class is closed.
（這班報名已額滿了。）

A : May I sign up the workshop?

B : Sorry, the workshop is already filled up to capacity, so you will need to register for next workshop.

A : 我可以報名工作坊嗎？

B : 抱歉，這工作坊已額滿，所以你需要報名下一梯工作坊。

補充

1. Sorry 用在告知別人不好的消息或做錯事情時使用。
2. May I..., please? 請問我可以⋯嗎？

▶▶ get the hang of sth. 學會某物

指很清楚掌握住某物的用法與訣竅。

A : I can't play the piano very well.

B : Don't worry. If you practice it every day, you'll get the hang of it soon.

A : 我鋼琴彈得不好。

B : 不要擔心，如果你每天練習，你很快就會學會。

▶▶ **get the most (out) of 充分利用**

使人或物做最有效的使用，而發揮最大功效。

A : I make sure to take careful notes, so that I can get the most out of my English lessons.

B : I think I should start doing that more often.

A : 我保證一定要認真記筆記，以便我能充分利用英文課程。

B : 我想我應該要開始多記筆記。

get the most (out) of = make the most (out) of

▶▶ in exchange for 交換

A : I helped Vivian learn English in exchange for her to teach me some Chinese.

B : How often do you two meet up?

A : 我幫薇薇安學英文，她教我一些中文作為交換。

B : 你們倆多久碰面一次呢？

▶▶ mess up 搞砸

A : I wish I could have more time to rehearse my play.

B : Take your time. You're not going to mess it up.

A : 我希望我能有更多的時間來排練我的戲劇。

B : 輕鬆點，你不會搞砸它的。

PART

(補充)

常用句型爲 This is your last chance, so don't mess up.（這是你最後機會，所以不要搞砸。）

▶▶ pick up 學習

(解說)

若 pick up 用在學習外語，是指強調自然學習且不費力地學會。

 : I think once I have more spare time, I'm going to pick up some English.

B : How much do lessons cost?

A : 我想一旦我有更多空閒的時間，我就會去學習一些英文。

B : 上課要多少錢呢？

▶▶ stick around 留下來

A : Do you want to stick around and learn something new?

B : I'd love to, but it's getting late.

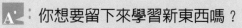

A：你想要留下來學習新東西嗎？

B：我很想啊，但是時間很晚了。

▶▶ take place 舉行

A：The training will take place next Friday.

B：There goes the barbecue.

A：這訓練將在下星期五舉行。

B：烤肉泡湯了。

take place = be held

03 工作溝通

(一) 電話

▶▶ **be back** 回來

: Do you know when he will be back?

: No, I am sorry. I don't know.

: 你知道他什麼時候會回來嗎？

: 抱歉，我不知道。

補充

I don't know. = I have no idea.

▶▶ **by telephone** 打電話

解說

為打電話或用電話的意思；by the telephone 在電話旁。

: Please see to it that you have to touch base with your clients regularly.

: Thank you for reminding me. I'll try to reach them by telephone.

A：請注意，你必須定期跟你的顧客聯繫。

B：謝謝你提醒我，我會試著用電話跟他們聯繫的。

補充

1. touch base with（聯繫）強調重新建立聯繫方式。
2. 電話場景，打電話常會說的句型有 Please call my cell phone.
  （請打我的手機。）I'll give you a buzz ／ call later.（待會打
  電話給你。）Please call me up.（請打電話給我。）

▶▶ be wanted on the phone
有某人的電話

A：You are wanted on the phone.

B：This is Tom speaking. May I ask who's calling, please?

A：找你的電話。

B：我是湯姆，請問誰找我嗎？

補充

類似句型：The phone's for you.（找你的電話。）We played phone tag.（我們互打電話找對方。／我們玩電話追逐遊戲。）

PART

▶▶ call back 回電話

A: Hi, Alice. Are you free to speak now?

B: Not really, I'm in a hurry. Can I call you back in a few minutes?

> **A:** 嗨！艾麗絲，你現在方便說話嗎？
>
> **B:** 不行，我正在忙，我可以幾分鐘後再回電話給你嗎？

▶▶ call for sb. 找某人

A: Amanda has been calling for you all afternoon. Why won't you speak to her?

B: We got into a fight, and I'm not ready to talk to her.

> **A:** 艾曼達整個下午一直打來找你，你為什麼不跟她說話呢？
>
> **B:** 我們吵架了，而我還沒準備好跟她說話。

call for sth. 預測什麼，如 The weather forecaster is calling for rain tomorrow. 天氣預報員預測明天有雨。

▶▶ come up 發生

A: Can I return your call later? Something has come up here.

B: Yes. Please let me know if you need any help.

A: 我可以稍後再回電話給你嗎？這裡發生一些事情。

B: 可以，如果你需要任何幫忙，請讓我知道。

▶▶ get the phone 接電話

A: Who gets the phone from an agent in China?

B: Peter.

A: 誰接到中國代理商的電話呢？

B: 彼得。

PART

▶▶ give sb. a call 給某人打電話

A : He is out of office right now.

B : Please give me a call as soon as he is back.

A : 他現在不在辦公室。

B : 他一回來，請立即打電話給我。

▶▶ hang up 掛斷電話

A : I have to hang up the phone because I've to get back to work now. Can I call you back later, OK?

B : Sure. I will be in office until noon.

A : 我必須掛斷電話，因為我現在得繼續工作。我能稍後再打電話給你嗎？

B : 當然可以，中午之前我都在辦公室。

電話場景中，有事要掛電話都會講 Gotta go.（我得走了。）或 I should go.（我得走了。）；gotta = got + to 的縮寫。

▶▶ hold on 別掛電話

A : Is Michelle there?

B : Hold on; let me see if she is around.

A : 蜜雪兒在嗎？

B : 別掛電話，讓我看一下她是否在附近。

▶▶ hold the line 不掛斷電話

A : I'll connect you. Please hold the line.

B : OK.

A : 我為你轉接，請你不要掛斷電話。

B : 好的。

PART

▶▶ I'm calling to + V 我打電話是為了

A : I'm calling to invite him to a party next week. Please call me back when he gets back.

B : OK, I will tell him to call you back.

A : 我打電話來是為了邀請他參加下週的派對，當他回來時，請他回我電話。

B : 沒問題，我會告訴他要回你電話。

類似的片語 I'm calling for + N 我打電話來是爲了。

▶▶ leave a message 留話／留言

A : May I leave a message?

B : Can you please hold on for a second while I get a pen?（或者可用此句來代替Hold on for a second, let me get a pen.等一下，讓我去拿筆。）

A : 請問我可以留言嗎？

B : 我去拿筆，你能等一下嗎？

▶▶ May I speak to..., please?

我想要找…

 : This is Business Center. How may I help you?

 : May I speak to the manager, please?

 這裡是商務中心，有什麼我可以為你效勞的嗎？

 我可以找經理嗎？

補充

「我想要找」類似的用法有 I'd like to talk to... = I am trying to reach...。

▶▶ on the phone 在講電話 / 在打電話

解說

on the phone 與 over the phone 的差別，on the phone 強調正在講電話，over the phone 強調透過工具來講電話。

 : This is Mary. May I speak to Mr. Brown?

 : He is on the phone. Will you hold?

：我是瑪麗，我要找布朗先生？

：他在講電話，你能等一下嗎？

補充

This is + 人（我是），指對方沒親眼看見對方，透過工具溝通；
I'm + 人（我是），指親眼看到對方，直接溝通。

▶▶ put sb. on hold 讓某人等

解說

強調擱置延期或暫停。

：Please do not put me on hold to take another call.

：Sorry, madam. I won't able to finish up the conversation with you and I'll call you later.

：你接到另一通電話，不要讓我等太久。

：抱歉，夫人，我將要結束跟你的對話，我等一下再回電給你。

補充

類似句型：I'm sorry to keep you waiting.（抱歉讓你久等了。）

 put through 接通（電話）／轉接（電話）

A: Could you connect me to extension number 111?

B: Sure. Just a moment, Mr. Peter. I'll put you through.

A: 你可以幫我轉接分機號碼111嗎？

B: 沒問題，彼得先生請稍等一下，我將為你轉接。

補充

轉接分機常用句型 Could I have extension 111, please?（請轉接分機 111，好嗎？）

 return sb.'s call 回某人電話

A: He just went out; he will be back in an hour.

B: Ask him to return my call when he comes back, please.

A : 他剛出去，他會在1小時後回來。
B : 他回來後，請叫他給我回個電話。

▶▶ Sure, go ahead. 當然可以.

A : She is not in. Could you call again in 10 minutes?

B : Sure, go ahead.

A : 她不在，你能在10分鐘後再打來嗎？
B : 當然可以。

▶▶ take a message 留言

A : He's not in. May I take a message?

B : Yes, please.

A : 他不在，我可以幫你留言嗎？
B : 好的，謝謝。

1

He's not in. = He is out. = He is not here. = He is not available.

▶▶ transfer sb.'s call 為某人轉接電話

A : Please hold on a second, while I transfer your call.

B : Thank you.

A : 請等一會，我為你轉接電話。

B : 謝謝你。

▶▶ who is calling 誰打來電話

A : How can I find out who is calling me?

B : You can use True Caller on your Android phone. The application can tell you the name and location of the caller.

A : 我如何查出誰打電話給我呢？

B : 你可以使用安卓手機上的True caller app軟體，這軟體可以告知你打電話者的姓名和地點。

PART

類似句型 Who's calling, please?（請問你是誰？）／ Who is this?
（這是什麼人？）

（二）會議

▶▶ Achilles' heel 唯一的致命弱點

來自希臘故事，Achilles 是刀槍不壞之身的英雄，唯一的弱點是
腳踝，在特洛伊戰爭時，任何武器都傷不了他，但被 Paris 射箭
擊中腳踝而喪命。

A': I want to ask you to make an oral presentation.

B': Sorry, that's my Achilles' heel.

A': 我想要你做一個口頭簡報。

B': 抱歉，那是我唯一的致命弱點。

讓某人做某事的句型 get ／ ask ／ make ／ let ／ send ／ have sb.
to do sth.

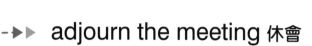

▶▶ adjourn the meeting 休會

A: When you're done; it's time to adjourn the meeting.

B: I'd like to make one more point.

> **A:** 你說完了，休會時間到了。
> **B:** 我還想要再說一點意見。

close the meeting 閉會。

▶▶ agree on ＋物 同意

指對某事有相同的看法。

A: Are we all agreed, ladies and gentlemen?

B: Yes, we all agree on the plan.

> **A:** 女士們，先生們，大家是否都同意了呢？
> **B:** 是的，我們全部都同意這計畫。

▶▶ agree up to 部分同意

強調部分的同意。

A : Do we all agree on the advertising campaign?

B : Yes. I agree up to a point but it depends on the advertisers.

> **A** : 我們全部都同意這廣告活動嗎?
>
> **B** : 是的,我部分同意,但是這要由廣告商來決定。

一般會議中,部分同意的句型有:
1. Yes, I partially agree, but... (是,我部分同意,但是…)
2. Yes, I suppose so, but... (是,我想也是,但是…)
3. Well, you've got a point there. (嗯,你找到了一個好的論據。)

▶▶ agree with sb. 同意

指跟某人觀點相同。

A：Do you agree with me about that point?

B：Yes, I quite agree with you.

A：你有同意我那個觀點嗎？

B：有，我非常同意你的觀點。

 補充

一般會議中，不同意的句型有：
1. No, I (strongly) disagree.〔不，我（強烈）不同意。〕
2. No, I don't agree with at all.（不，我根本就不同意你的意見。）
3. Well, I don't know.（嗯，我不知道。）
4. Well, I think it depends.（嗯，我想看情況。）

▶▶ **as soon as 一…就…**

A：When did the meeting begin?

B：As soon as the host arrived.

A：會議什麼時候開始？

B：主持人一抵達就開始。

▶▶ at once 同時

 : Can you make it to the fair tonight?

B : Sorry, I have a meeting and cannot be in two places at once.

A : 你今晚能來展覽會嗎？

B : 抱歉，我有一個會議，而不能同時出現在兩個地方。

補充

常用句型 To delete multiple messages at once.（要立刻刪除重複訊息。）

▶▶ be held 舉行

A : Where will the seminar be held?

B : The seminar will take place at the meeting room.

A : 研討會將在哪裡舉行呢？

B : 研討會將在會議室舉行。

> **補充**
>
> be held = take place

▶▶ be served 供應

A : I'm a little hungry. I didn't eat the breakfast this morning.

B : Please be patient for a while. Refreshments will be served during the intermission.

A : 我有點餓，我今早沒吃早餐。

B : 請忍耐一下，三明治在中場休息時間會供應。

▶▶ brand storytelling 品牌故事

A : What's the main point of this meeting?

B : In my opinion, it is to discuss the brand story-telling.

A : 會議要點是什麼呢？

B : 我認為是要討論品牌故事。

一般要表達自己的觀點或立場的常用句型有：
1. In my opinion,...（我認爲）
2. I think...（我認爲）
3. Personally,...（在我看來）
4. As far as I'm concerned,...（在我看來）

▶▶ break it down for sb. 為某人詳細說明

break down 有「分解」或「分成若干部分」的意思，The meeting breaks down into subdiscussions.（這會議分成不同種類的小討論會。）而 break it down for sb. 直譯爲「爲某人把它分解成若干部分」，這樣就比較好分析與明瞭，而引申爲「爲某人詳細說明」。break down 也有「故障」的意思，指機器因被分解就會故障，不能運行，如 The computer breaks down.（電腦故障。）

A: I don't understand what the point is.

B: I will break it down for you after the meeting.

A: 我不明白重點是什麼。

B: 在會議之後，我會爲你詳細說明。

不明白常用句型 It's above me. / It's beyond me. / It's over my head. / I can't follow what you said. / I'm lost.

▶▶ elaborate on 詳細說明

A : Can someone please elaborate on this problem?

B : I think I can briefly introduce this problem.

A : 請問有人可以詳細說明這個問題嗎？

B : 我想我可以簡要介紹這個問題。

▶▶ get down to business 著手做正事

A : Stop joking. Let's get down to business.

B : All right. We are going to discuss your plans today.

A : 不要開玩笑，讓我們開始做正事吧。

B : 好的，今天我們將討論你的計畫。

PART

get started 開始

A: Shall we get started?

B: As soon as everyone arrived.

A：我們開始好嗎？
B：只要每個人一到就開始。

hold water 說得通

主要用在理論與論證相關的否定句中，一般翻譯爲「說得通」
或「可行的」。

A: Does your theory hold water?

B: I have a considerable amount of proof and data to back it up.

A：你的理論說得通嗎？
B：我有相當多的證據和資料來做佐證。

▶▶ **how often 多久一次**

只問多長的時間，指問頻率。

A : How often do you have a meeting?

B : At least once a month.

A : 你們多久開會一次？

B : 至少一月一次。

補充

how soon 多快 / 多久之後，比如 How soon will the meeting begin?（這會議多久之後開始？）

▶▶ **I can't agree more. 我非常支持**

A : Are you for this plan?

B : I can't agree more.

A : 你支持這計畫嗎？

B : 我非常支持。

PART

in agreement 同意

解說

意見一致。

A: Does the client agree with the price?

B: She nodded her head in agreement.

A: 這位顧客有同意這價格嗎?

B: 她點頭表示同意。

補充

常用句型為 Are we in agreement about the changes to the contract?
(我們一致同意修改契約嗎?)

in favor of 贊成

A: Are we all for this decision?

B: Yes, we are all in favor of this decision.

A: 我們全部都贊成這個決定嗎?

B: 對,我們全部都贊成這個決定。

(補充)

贊成常用句型有 You said it. ／ By all means. ／ You bet. ／ Sure thing. ／ Go ahead. ／ Cool. ／ I don't wonder. ／ It couldn't be better. ／ I see eye to see with you.

 ## inside out 非常熟悉

(解說)

直譯為「由裡到外」的意思，如 I sometimes wear my socks inside out. 我有時會把我的襪子穿反了，有引申為「非常熟悉」的意思。

A: Are you prepared for the presentation tomorrow?

B: I'm prepared for that. I know the material inside out.

A: 你準備好明天的簡報了嗎？

B: 我準備好了，我非常熟悉這些內容。

▶▶ **lucky break** 運氣很好

(解)(說)

指沒有預料到的好運氣。

 : The boss postponed the meeting until next week.

 : Great. Sounds like we caught a lucky break.

 : 老闆把會議延到下週。
 : 太棒了,聽起來我們的運氣很好。

▶▶ **move on** 接著

(解)(說)

指結束某項活動後,改做其他事情。

 : OK, then let's move on the next item on the agenda.

 : Good idea.

 : 好的,那麼讓我們接著議程上的下一個項目。
 : 好主意。

▶▶ off the point 離題

 : Shall we get back to the main point?

B : Sure. I think we're getting off the point, too.

A : 我們能回到正題嗎？

B : 可以，我也覺得我們正在離題。

補充

to the point 切題 / 正題。

▶▶ put off 延後

 : I think it would have been better if the meeting was put off until next week.

B : I thought we were all pretty much in agreement.

A : 我想如果會議延後到下週，那將會更好。

B : 我想我們全部都會很同意。

補充

put off = delay = postpone

▶▶ **put up sb.'s hand 舉手**

A : Who will oppose the proposal? Please put your hand up.

B : I'm in favor of the proposal.

A : 誰反對這提案,請舉手。

B : 我是贊成這個提案。

 補充

1. put up sb.'s hand = raise sb.'s hand
2. 在對話中,若第二個人不明確回答第一個人的問題,就是第二個人反對第一個人的問題,而第二個人回覆常用句型有 Are you kidding? ／ Who says that? ／ Who says so?

▶▶ **preside over 主持**

A : I'm not satisfied by the way you presided over the discussions today.

B : How so? I thought it went well.

A : 我不滿意你今天主持討論的方式。

B : 為什麼你這麼說呢?我認為它進行得很好。

preside over = handle

▶▶ run out of time 沒時間

run out of 是「用光」、「用完」的意思，如 I just ran out of gas. 我剛用完了汽油；而 run out of time 直譯為「用光了時間」，引申為「沒時間」。

A: Miss Tina, We are running out of time. Can we have your report now?

B: Of course.

A: 蒂娜小姐，我們快沒時間了，你現在可以報告了嗎？

B: 當然可以。

▶▶ sidetracked 偏離主題

指分散思路而轉變了話題或目標。

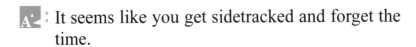
A : It seems like you get sidetracked and forget the time.

B : You are right. The time is so short. So, I'll stick to the main problem from now on.

A : 似乎好像你偏離主題和忘記時間。

B : 你說得對，時間很短，所以從現在開始我會回到正題。

▶▶ **stick to** 捉住／堅守

指黏住什麼事情而不放棄。

A : Remember, stick to the main point and don't say anything irrelevant.

B : I think we're getting off the point here. So please be quiet or say something supportive.

A : 記住，捉住要點，不要說些不相關的話。

B : 我想我們離題了，所以請安靜點或說些有建設性的話。

▶▶ take minutes 做會議紀錄

minute 為「分鐘」的意思，其複數 minutes 為「會議紀錄」。

A : Who is going to take the meeting minutes this time?

B : This time it's my turn.

A : 這一次誰做會議紀錄呢？

B : 這次輪到我了。

note 與 minutes 都有記錄的意思，take notes 指大多數人主動自己做記錄，而 take minutes 是強調一個人做紀錄；其常用句型有 Can someone volunteer to take minutes today?（今天有人可以志願做會議紀錄嗎？）

▶▶ too good to be true 好到難以置信

too...to... 的句型意思為「太…所以不（能／要）」，too good to be true 直譯為「太好所以不可能是真的」。

A : I cannot believe the boss cancelled the meeting.

B : If it sounds too good to be true, it probably is.

A : 我不敢相信老闆取消了會議。

B : 如果它聽起來是好到難以置信，你最好還是別信。

▶▶ turn to 開始討論

A : How about taking a break before we turn to the second problem?

B : Sounds good. I really can't wait another minute.

A : 在我們開始討論第二個問題之前，我們休息一下如何？

B : 聽起來不錯，我簡直連一分鐘也等不及了。

▶▶ wrap up 結束

指能得到結論的結束。

A : When will you be home for dinner?

B : The meeting is just about to wrap up, so I should be home in roughly 30 minutes.

> **A :** 你什麼時候回家吃晚飯呢？
>
> **B :** 這會議準備結束了，所以我大約在30分後到家。

(補)(充)

be about to 即將。

(三) 產品

▶▶ arrive at 到達

at 介詞用在小地方，in 介詞用在大地方。

A : When will the shipment arrive at New York?

B : At noon tomorrow.

PART

A：這批貨物何時到達紐約？

B：明天中午。

▶▶ ## be dedicated to 致力於

A：Sony is dedicated to producing innovative smartphones.

B：That's because the Sony smartphone offers multifarious functionality. It's made for entertainment not for education.

A：索尼致力於生產創新型智慧型手機。

B：那是因為索尼智慧型手機提供五花八門的功能，它是為娛樂而不是為教育而製造的。

 補充

1. be dedicated to = be devoted to。
2. multifarious 各式各樣的。
3. be made for 為…製造。

be disappointed by sth.
因某事感到失望

be disappointed with ／ in + sb. ／ sths. 對某人／某事感到失望，其中 with 較常用，用 with 表示心中感到失望，而用 in 表示失望藏在心中。

A： Please, just tell me how I can help you.

B： I'm really disappointed by the service recently.

A： 請告訴我，要我怎樣幫助你。

B： 我最近對你們的服務真的感到失望。

be pleased with 滿意於

指喜歡而感到滿意。

A： How can I help you?

B： You've done it already. I'm so pleased with your service.

：我該怎樣幫你呢？

B'：你已經做了，我很滿意你的服務。

補充

一般店員打招呼口語有：
1. May I help you? 我能幫你嗎？
2. Is there anything I can do for you? 有什麼事我可以為你服務嗎？
3. Is there anything else I can help you with? 還有什麼事我能幫你服務嗎？

▶▶ be released 推出

A'：Do you know when the product will be released?

B'：If there are no problems, the product will be launched next month.

A'：你知道這產品何時推出嗎？

B'：如果沒有問題，這產品將在下月推出。

be released = be launched

▶▶ be short for 縮寫

A: What's the cell phone brand HTC stand for?

B: It is short for "High Tech Computer".

A: 手機品牌HTC是代表什麼？
B: 它是高科技電腦的縮寫。

▶▶ be worth + N / Ving 價值

A: For all I know, the seller could be trying to scam me.

B: I think the item is not worth that much. Maybe you should go somewhere else.

A: 據我所知，這賣家可能想騙我錢。
B: 我想這項商品沒有值那麼多錢，或許你應該去別的地方。

PART

▶▶ **call on** 拜訪

指短暫的拜訪。

> A : Is there anything I can do for you?
>
> B : I just wanted to call on and thank you for using our products and services.

> A : 有什麼事情我可以為您效勞的嗎?
> B : 我只是拜訪一下,並謝謝你使用我們的產品與服務。

補充
call on = call in = come by = drop by = drop in

▶▶ **carry around** 攜帶

指隨身攜帶。

> A : Do you mind if you carry around the product catalogue to my office?
>
> B : Never mind.

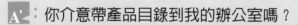

A：你介意帶產品目錄到我的辦公室嗎？

B：不介意。

▶▶ count for much 關係重大

A：We don't focus so much on special products for elderly people because it doesn't count for much.

B：We should pay close attention to beauty and practicality.

A：我們不要把太多焦點放在老人的特殊產品上，因為它重要性不大。

B：我們應該密切注意美觀與實用性。

▶▶ fill sb. in 詳細告訴某人

A：Have you received our new product catalogue?

B：No, but can you fill me in?

A：你有收到我們新的產品目錄嗎？

B：沒有，但是你能詳細告訴我嗎？

補充

fill sb. in on = tell sb. the details

▶▶ **have sb.'s word** 保證

A: You have my word that I will be provided with a high quality service.

B: That's what you said last time.

A: 我保證我會提供一個高品質的服務給你。

B: 你上次也這麼說。

▶▶ **in one piece** 完整無缺的

A: It's important that the product is in one piece.

B: You are right. There is no damage to the design.

A: 重要的是產品完美無缺。

B: 你說得對，圖案沒有任何損傷。

▶▶ make up sb.'s mind 做出決定

解說
指面臨選擇或意見，而終於下定決心。

: Have you decided which product to buy?

B: Not yet. It's hard to make up my mind.

A: 你決定要買哪一種產品嗎？

B: 還沒決定，我很難做出決定。

▶▶ no longer 不再

A: I wonder what the problem is. She will no longer support the brand.

B: That's because she get bad service like that.

A: 我想知道問題是什麼，她將不再支持這品牌。

B: 那是因為她得到那樣差的服務。

補充

no longer = no more

▶▶ off the market 撤出市場

解說

指脫離市場或引爆市場。

：Our competition is dropping their prices. How should you respond?

：I can't help, but I think this product will be taken off the market.

：我們的競爭者正在降價,我們應該如何反應呢?

：我幫不了忙,但是我想這項產品會撤出市場。

補充

類似片語 on the market(在市場上),其主詞必須為物,如 The new products are not yet on the market.(這些新產品尚未上市。),若其主詞為人,其意思為「單身」,如 I'm on the market.(我單身。)

▶▶ out of stock 缺貨

解說

指商店沒有貨。

A: Did you talk to your distributor?

B: No, the product is out of stock while buying. What a pain in the neck.

A: 你有跟你的批發商說嗎？

B: 沒有，當我要買時，這產品缺貨，是多麼討厭的事啊。

in stock 有現貨。

▶▶ **place an order 訂購**

A: Is there a problem, Sir?

B: I placed an order for an organic fruit basket last week, but it's not yet arrived.

A: 先生，有問題嗎？

B: 我上週訂購有機水果一籃，但是還沒有送到。

▶▶ put a lot of time into 在…花很多時間

A: I counsel you to give up the research.

B: But I put a lot of time into it.

A: 我建議你放棄這項研究。

B: 我已花了很多時間在上面了。

put a lot of time into = put a lot of hours into = put in a lot of time = put in a lot of hours

▶▶ rush order 緊急訂單

A: I have a rush order. May you help me out?

B: I'm always happy to help out a friend.

A: 我有一個緊急訂單,你能幫忙我嗎?

B: 我總是樂意幫朋友解決問題。

▶▶ track an order 查訂單

A : Can you please help me track an order I placed with you last month? I haven't received my order yet.

B : Certainly, Sir. You may track your order by visiting our website.

A : 你能幫我查一筆我上個月和你們訂的貨？我還沒收到我的貨。

B : 先生，當然可以，你可以訪問我們的網站來查你的訂單。

place an order 下訂單。

PART

04 工作表現

（一）工作情況

be finished 完成

A : When will the advertising plans be finished?

B : By Thursday, I hope.

A : 廣告規劃何時會完成？

B : 我希望在星期四之前完成。

補充
做完常用片語 be done with ／ be finished with ／ be through with，這些片語要以主詞是人為主。

beyond sb. 無法理解

解說
直譯為「超出某人的能力」，引申為「無法理解」。

A : Why would he make such a poor decision?

B : It's beyond me.

A：他為什麼會做出如此差的決定呢？

B：我無法理解。

▶▶ break up 分工

A：There are six of us in the group, and six parts of the assignment.

B：I think we should break up the project, and each do one task.

A：在小組裡，我們有六個人，而作業有六部分。

B：我想我們應該把專題分工，每人做一個部分。

▶▶ bust sb.'s ass 非常賣力

直譯為「打某人的屁股」，引申「非常賣力、努力工作」。此片語為非正式用法，其正式用法為 work hard。

A : I have been busting my ass for three days studying for this marketing proposal, so I'd better perform well.

B : Don't worry so much. I am sure you are more prepared than most of the other colleagues.

A : 為這次行銷提案，我一直非常賣力地準備了3天，所以我最好能表現的很好。

B : 不要擔心這麼多，我相信你比其他大部分的同事做了更多的準備。

▶▶ come by 得到

強調占有或取得；此片語也有「過來」（指拜訪或串門子）的意思，如 I invited him to come by for some coffee. 我邀請他過來喝咖啡。

A : The job is really interesting. The pay is decent and the benefits are excellent. I am interested in the job.

B : But the job is hard to come by.

：這工作非常有趣，薪水合理且福利很好，我對這工作很感興趣。

：但是這工作很難得到。

補充

類似句型 I got the sale.（我拿到這筆交易。）

▶▶ **come into** 得到

解說

此片語還有二種意義，第一種意義是「繼承」，指強調某人死後，而得到某人的財產或名號，I come into possession of a large fortune after my grandfather died.（我祖父死後，我繼承了大筆財富。）；第二種意義是「進入」，Come into the conference room, we've got to discuss the budget table.（進來會議室，我們得討論預算表。）

：Wow, new car, new house. Did you come into a millions contract with a client recently?

：Believe it or not, I won the state lottery.

：哇，新車，新房子，你最近得到客戶數百萬的合約嗎？

：信不信由你，我中了州彩券。

083

▶▶ Come on, be serious 拜託，認真一點

A : I am going to look for a new job.

B : Come on, be serious. Your current job is good pay.

> **A** : 我正在尋找新工作。
> **B** : 拜託，認真一點，你目前工作待遇很好。

▶▶ come up with 想出

強調想出的計畫或答案是有創意性的。

A : I need to come up with an idea for my design project, but I can't think of anything.

B : Just think about any issue you're interested in, and write about that.

> **A** : 我需要想出我設計方案構想，但是我想不出任何東西。
> **B** : 想想你感興趣的任何議題，然後寫下來。

> **補充**
>
> 常用句型有 I can't come up with any ideas.（我想不出任何點子。）；I can't think of anything to say.（我想不出要說什麼。）

▶▶ cope with 應付

A： How can you cope with going to school and working full-time?

B： It is difficult, but I just try to manage my time well.

> **A：** 你如何應付上學和全職工作呢？
> **B：** 很困難，但我只不過盡量有效地管理我的時間。

▶▶ do sb.'s best 盡全力

A： Please see to it that you finish the first part of the project by Thursday.

B： Ok, I'll do my best.

> **A：** 請注意，你在星期四前要完成你專題的第一部分。
> **B：** 好的，我會盡全力。

補充

1. do sb.'s best = try sb.'s best
2. Please see to it that + 子句（請注意），而 see to 有「負責料理」的意思，比如 Don't worry. I'll see to the rest.（別擔心，我會負責剩下的。）

▶▶ drop off 送

A: I want to drop the documents off at Mary's office. Do you need any help?

B: No, that's all right.

A: 我要送這些檔案到瑪麗辦公室，你需要任何的幫忙嗎？

B: 沒有，沒有什麼事。

 補充

常用句型 I can drop you off on my way home.（我回家路上可以順便送你。）24 / 7 drop off service.（整年無休遞送服務。），其 24 / 7 唸法為 twenty four seven.

▶▶ focus on 專心

指對某事或做某事時，予以聚焦注意力。

A : Have you come up with a solution to this problem yet?

B : Look, I cannot focus on it if you guys keep bugging me. All I'm asking for is a little room to think.

A : 你有想出解決這個問題的辦法了嗎？

B : 聽著，如果你們持續打擾我，我就不能專心，我所要求的只是一個小的可以思考的空間。

1. bug 打擾。
2. focus on = concentrate on

▶▶ get done 完成

A : How much did you get done?

B : I feel I've done very little.

A : 你完成了多少呢？

B : 我覺得我完成很少。

▶▶ get down to business 開始工作

A : After we have dinner, we will then get down to business.

B : There is still an hour before dinner is ready, so maybe we can discuss a little about the details of merger now.

A : 吃完晚飯後，我們再開始工作。

B : 晚飯做好前，還要一小時，所以或許我們現在可以討論一下合併的細節。

get down to business = get to work

▶▶ have a difficult time 做某事上有困難

後面要接動名詞。

A : I am having a difficult time doing my job.

B : Why don't you come by after work, and we can work on it together?

A : 我在處理我的工作上有困難。

B : 你為什麼不下班後過來，我們可以一起解決它呢？

 補充

1. 工作上談到發生困難，其他常用句型 I have trouble with... / I'm having a problem... / I'm having a hard time with...
2. 工作上遇到困難，解決態度要正向積極樂觀，所以常用句型有 Don't give up.（不要放棄。）Stick with it.（堅持下去。）

▶▶ ins and outs 細節

A : How's your new job going?

B : I already know the ins and outs of the electronics business, so I am adjusting quite well.

A : 你的新工作如何？

B : 我已經知道電子商務的細節，所以我適應得十分良好。

PART

補充

ins and outs = details

▶▶ keep at it 繼續保持

A : You have really been doing a great job at work lately.

B : Thanks for the compliment, sir. I'll be sure to keep at it.

A : 你最近在工作上真的做得很好。

B : 先生，謝謝你的稱讚，我一定會繼續保持下去。

▶▶ outdo oneself 超出水準

A : What did you think of Lisa's design?

B : She really outdid herself this time.

A : 你認為莉莎的設計如何？

B : 她這次表現真是超出水準。

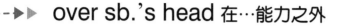

▶▶ over sb.'s head 在…能力之外

A : Do you read French?

B : It's over my head.

A : 你看得懂法語嗎？
B : 它超出我的能力之外。

▶▶ put the heat on sb. 對某人施壓

直譯為「增加熱」，引申對某人威脅或強迫。

A : I heard the boss is tough and picky.

B : He usually puts the heat on employees to raise their levels of thinking.

A : 我聽說老闆很嚴格和挑剔。
B : 他經常對員工施壓來提升他們的思想層面。

▶▶ put into 把⋯翻譯成

A : Why don't you put it in plain Chinese?

B : I don't know how to put it into Chinese.

A : 你為什麼不用簡單易懂的中文說它呢？

B : 我不知道如何把它翻譯成中文。

▶▶ make sense 有道理

指合理的邏輯和解釋；此片語常用句型有 It doesn't make sense.（沒意義。）

A : Jill said that she's moving to Chicago at the end of November.

B : That doesn't make any sense. She told me she was working in New York.

A : 吉兒說她在11月底要搬到芝加哥去。

B : 那沒有任何道理，她告訴我她要去紐約工作。

▶▶ stress out 壓力太大

stress 壓力。

A : I'm nervous that I need to hand in a design portfolio next week.

B : Don't stress out. Just do one thing at a time.

A : 我很緊張，我下週要繳交一份設計作品集。

B : 不要壓力太大，一次只做一件事。

▶▶ work sb. to death 拚命工作

形容做到勞累死亡，就是拚命工作的意思。

A : My boss has been working me to death.

B : Maybe it's time to take a vacation.

A : 我的老闆一直讓我拚命工作。

B : 或許該是度假的時候到了。

PART

▶▶ work sb.'s tail off 拚命工作

A : I plan to work my tail off getting the chances of promotion.

B : You'll have to kiss a lot of corporate butt, to become an executive.

A : 我打算拚命工作，來得到升遷的機會。

B : 要成為一位主管，你得拍許多上司的馬屁。

kiss butt 奉承，拍馬屁。

(二) 工作忙

▶▶ around the clock 日夜不停

A : I have a deadline coming up. I work around the clock now.

B : So when exactly are you going to finish this job?

A : 我有一個工作的最後期限即將來臨，我現在都日夜不停的工作。

B : 所以你到底什麼時候能完成這項工作呢？

補充

常用句型 It is due by Monday.（星期一到期。）

▶▶ be busy (with) + Ving 忙

：I've been so busy with working since I got transferred.

B:：I think it's time to take a vacation. Let's go somewhere and have fun.

：自從我調職後，我一直忙於工作。

B:：我想度假的時間到了，讓我們去一些地方玩一玩。

補充

很忙常用句型 I have a tight schedule.（我的行程很緊。）／ I need to check my schedule ／ calendar.（我需要看一下我的行程表／日曆。）／ My schedule is tight.（我的行程很緊。）／ I'm tied up in work ／ meeting.（我正忙著工作／開會。）；很忙常用片語 be in the middle of ／ up to sb.'s neck ／ eyes in work.

▶▶ squeeze in 擠壓

 解說

指推壓某人或某物，而擠壓出東西來。

A : Anyway, may you squeeze me in sometime to-day? We have to go over the things at once.

B : That's for sure.

A : 無論如何，你今天可以擠壓出一些時間給我嗎？
我們必須立刻檢查這些事情。

B : 當然沒問題。

▶▶ stay up 熬夜

A : Why do you stay up so late?

B : I have a deadline to meet.

A : 為什麼你熬夜到這麼晚呢？

B : 我有一個期限快到了，要趕工。

常用句型 If worst comes to worse, we'll stay up all night.（如果最壞的情況發生，我們準備整晚熬夜。）

▶▶ take up 占用

指時間、空間或精力上的占用。

A: I'm really sorry to take up so much of your time.

B: Never mind.

A: 我很抱歉占用你如此多的時間。

B: 不要緊。

Never mind. = I don't mind at all.

(三) 行銷

▶▶ a deal's a deal. 說話算話

交易就是交易，就是照合約辦事，來達成交易，強調要遵守信用。

A: You told me if I brought in new clients, you'd give me the commission, and a deal's a deal.

B: I will give you the commission but you just have to wait until I get bonus.

A: 你告訴我如果我帶新客戶來，你會給我佣金，說話要算話。

B: 我會給你佣金，但是你必須等我拿到獎金。

▶▶ aside from 除⋯以外

A: When do you have time to go over the survey results over again?

B: Aside from Friday, any day is fine with me.

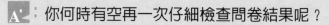

> **A** ：你何時有空再一次仔細檢查問卷結果呢？
>
> **B** ：除星期五以外，哪一天都行。

▶▶ be made of 由…構成

A ： What's the marketing plan made of?

B ： It is made of three critical components: communication, promotion, brand awareness.

> **A** ：這行銷計畫是由什麼構成的呢？
>
> **B** ：它是由溝通、促銷與品牌知名度等三個重要部分構成的。

be made of = be make out of

▶▶ be successful in 成功的

A ： The sale is down last season.

B ： But recently the company's advertising is successful in attracting customers to buy our product immediately.

PART

A：上一季銷售量下降。

B：但是最近的公司廣告立即成功的吸引消費者購買我們的產品。

▶▶ come a long way 取得很大進展

直譯為「走很長一段路」也就是「遠道而來」的意思，如 They came a long way to see me.（他們遠道前來看我。）；同時也引申為有了很大的進步或進展。

A：I saw your advertising campaign on Facebook. It's great.

B：Thanks. I think I have come a long way this time.

A：我在臉書上看到你的廣告活動，它很棒。

B：謝謝，我想我這次取得了很大進展。

▶▶ come from 來自某處

A: Where is the marketing information coming from?

B: It comes from the marketing research done.

A: 這行銷資料是從哪裡來的呢？
B: 行銷資料是來自已完成的市場研究調查。

▶▶ figure out 弄清楚

就是明白或理解某事。

A: My salesperson can't seem to explain the current trend in the market.

B: I think you are clever to figure that out.

A: 我的銷售人員似乎不能解釋現今市場的流行趨勢。
B: 我想你很聰明，應該能弄清楚這個現象。

▶▶ high style 高品質的生活

A: Once my invention is patented, I'll be living in high style.

B: But first, you'll have to market the product, and be able to sell it.

A: 一旦我的發明取得專利權,我將會過著高品質的生活。

B: 但是首先你得推銷這項產品,才能賣掉它。

▶▶ make use of 利用

A: How to attract more consumers to purchase our products?

B: We are supposed to make use of the mobile apps to marketing.

A: 如何吸引更多消費者來購買我們的產品?

B: 我們應該利用行動應用程式來行銷。

be supposed to 常用句型 It's supposed to be..., but it turned out to be... （原來應該…，可是結果卻…）

▶▶ **put a lot of time into** 在…花很多時間

A: I counsel you to give up the marketing plan.

B: It is a difficult plan, and I put a lot of time into it.

A: 我建議你放棄這項行銷計畫。

B: 它是一個很困難的專案，而且我已花了很多時間在上面了。

put a lot of time into = put a lot of hours into = put in a lot of time = put in a lot of hours

05 公司

(一) 公務處理

▶▶ **answer sb.'s question** 回答某人問題

A: I do hope I have answered your questions. I think I've told you everything I know.

B: Thanks very much. I really appreciate your help.

A: 我真的希望我有回答到你的問題,我想我已經告訴你我所知道的一切。

B: 非常謝謝你,我真的感謝你的幫忙。

▶▶ **By all means.** 當然可以

A: We need to deliver some documents to a company. Can you come by and pick them up?

B: By all means.

我們需要遞送一些檔案給一間公司，你可以過來取它們嗎？

B: 當然可以。

補充

deliver 與 send 都有「送出」的意義，其用法差別：deliver 是直接把東西交到某人手中，send 是透過安排把東西送到對方手中。

▶▶ count on 信任

A: I really appreciate you telling me about your thoughts.

B: You are welcome. I know I can count on you.

A: 我很感謝你告訴我你的想法。

B: 別客氣，我知道我可以信任你。

1. count on = rely on = trust
2. You are welcome. = Not at all. = Don't mention it. = No problem.

▶▶ Don't mention it. 別客氣

 : What about a coffee?

 : Don't mention it. （用這句回答也可以 That would be nice. 那太好了。）

 : 來一杯咖啡如何？

 : 別客氣。

補充

1. What about...? = How about...? = Would you like...（你認為如何）
2. 咖啡相關片語有 coffee break（喝咖啡時間）、black coffee（黑咖啡）、white coffee（加牛奶的咖啡）

▶▶ get back to 回覆

解說

事後的回覆。

 : How soon can you get back to me?

 : It depends.

 : 你要多久才能回覆我呢？

 : 看情況。

補充

常用句型有 Please get back to me ASAP.（請你盡快回覆我。）

▶▶ give...a hand 幫忙

 : Well, then, do you want to give me a hand?

B : Yes.

 : 嗯，那麼你想幫忙嗎？

B : 對啊。

▶▶ give sb. trouble 麻煩某人

 : I am sorry to give you trouble.

B : Do not say that. It's no trouble at all.

 : 我很抱歉麻煩你。

B : 不要這樣說，一點也不麻煩。

補充

give sb. trouble = put sb. to trouble 麻煩某人，打擾某人。

PART

▶▶ go over 重新檢視

含有用心仔細檢查與思考的意思。

A: Could you go over the main points with me again?

B: I'd be glad to.

A: 你可以跟我再重新檢視要點嗎?
B: 我很樂意。

(補)(充)
請求幫助句型有 Could you...? / Could I...?

▶▶ jot down 記下

指草草記下,而 write down 則是記下。

A: Could you please jot me down for a conference call line in the notebook?

B: Of course, no problem.

：你能幫我在這本筆記簿記下電話會議的對話嗎？

：當然可以，沒問題。

▶▶ no doubt 沒有懷疑

：I always have a way of getting things done for you.

：I have no doubt.

：我總是有辦法為你解決問題。

：我沒有懷疑。

補充

no doubt = to be sure = without doubt，而 No Doubt 也是美國搖滾樂界的一個團隊，流行在 80 年代末到 90 年代中期，女主唱 Gwen Stefani 是樂隊焦點人物。

▶▶ no matter what 不管怎樣

解說

no matter what = whatever, no matter what 要跟有主詞＋動詞的句子在一起，而 whatever 無此限制。

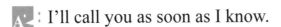

A : I'll call you as soon as I know.

B : All right. Call me no matter what.

A : 我一有消息就會給你打電話。

B : 好的，你不管怎樣都要打電話給我。

▶▶ **on the contrary** 相反地

A : Thanks for your help.

B : It doesn't matter; on the contrary, it is my pleasure.

A : 謝謝你的幫忙。

B : 不客氣，相反地，它是我的榮幸。

▶▶ **red tape** 繁瑣公事程序

 解說

指官僚作風造成繁瑣的程序，就是繁文縟節。

A : When are you going to finish this job?

B : I have no idea. The red tape has delayed the job.

A : 你何時會完成這工作？

B : 我不知道，這繁瑣公事程序已推延了這個工作。

▶▶ **talk over** 討論

解說

指雙方都很坦誠的交談。

A : Would you like to come to my office and discuss this matter?

B : I'd like to drop by next Monday to talk over our matter.

A : 你想要過來我的辦公室討論這個問題嗎？

B : 我想要下星期一過來討論我們的問題。

PART

▶▶ **wade through 完成**

解 說

指辛苦的完成；go through with + sth. 完成，指把心中決定的事，進行到底。

 The work seems simple enough, but there is so much red tape to wade through.

 Sure, but I'm still unclear about a few things.

A : 這工作似乎很簡單，但是卻有很多繁瑣公事程序需要完成。

B : 沒錯，但是我仍然對幾件事情不是很清楚。

(二) 員工

▶▶ # a long way off 差的很遠

A : I wish I could become a famous game developer.

B : In your dreams. You are still a long way off.

> **A** : 我希望我能變成有名的遊戲開發師。
>
> **B** : 別做夢,你還差的很遠。

▶▶ # a way out of the mess
一個擺脫麻煩辦法

mess 在這兒指不好的事情,常用來當困境或麻煩。

A : My boss asked me to stay late, but I have a personal appointment. I need to find a way out of the mess.

B : Why don't you just tell your boss you need to watch your baby brother tonight?

A：我的老闆要求我留晚一點，但是我有一個私人的約會，我得找到一個辦法擺脫麻煩。

B：你為什麼不告訴你的老闆，你今晚得照顧你的弟弟呢？

▶▶ an act of faith 信心行動

解說

指行為或行動呈現出相信某人或某事，強調是有安全感的信任。

A：Moving to Taiwan required an act of faith.

B：The first three months were difficult to adjust, but now I feel right at home.

A：到臺灣發展需要信心行動。

B：前三個月很難適應，但是現在我感覺像在家裡一樣自在。

▶▶ after work 下班後

A : Would you like to do something after work tonight?

B : What did you have in mind?

A : 今晚下班後，你想要做什麼呢？

B : 你有什麼想法嗎？

類似的片語有 after school 放學後，after class 下課後。

▶▶ be appointed to 擔任

A : Who will be appointed to the position of manager?

B : As far as I know, maybe it's Tom.

A : 誰會被指定擔任經理的職位呢？

B : 據我所知，可能是湯姆。

▶▶ be regarded as 被視為

A: Employees are regarded as an asset and not a liability to the company.

B: Sure. Most of the top companies treat their workforce as an asset rather than liabilities.

A: 員工對於公司而言是資產不是負債。

B: 沒錯,大部分的優秀公司都把員工勞動力當作資產而不是負債。

▶▶ be suited for 適合

A: How is the new staff?

B: I feel he isn't suited for the job and maybe will leave soon.

A: 新來的員工怎麼樣?

B: 我覺得他不適合這份工作,可能很快就會離職。

how + be 動詞,指問狀況或好壞,How is the new plan going?(這新計畫如何呢?)

▶▶ **big deal** 大事情

解說

物爲主詞時，意思爲「重大的事情」；人爲主詞時，意思爲「名人」、「大人物」的意思，如 Connery is a big deal in the spotlight. 康納利是演藝圈的名人。

 : I can't believe I was promoted to manager.

 : Wow, that's a big deal.

A : 我無法相信我獲升爲經理。

B : 哇，那是一件大事情。

▶▶ **blind luck** 純屬運氣

解說

只強調非常好的運氣。

 : How in the world did Evan get a job as an Executive for Intel?

 : Blind luck really. He was at a restaurant and helped someone who was choking. That someone just happened to be the CEO of Intel.

PART

：伊文到底是怎樣得到英特爾經理主管的工作呢？

：純屬運氣，他在餐廳幫助某個快窒息的人，那某人正巧是英特爾的執行長。

補 充

常用句型為 It's blind luck for me.（我是純屬運氣。）

▶▶ blow it 徹底搞砸

：Jennifer is giving me another chance.

：You'd better not blow it this time.

：珍妮佛給我另一個機會。

：你最好這次不要搞砸它。

▶▶ boss sb. around 對某人呼來喚去

解 說

指像老闆一樣，指揮或差遣某人。

A : I am sick of a colleague always bossing me around.

B : Why don't you tell your director to have her stop?

A : 我厭倦某位同事總是對我呼來喚去。

B : 你為何不告訴你主管來制止她呢？

▶▶ brace yourself 做好準備

A : Oh, my god! The stock market is bearish and the economy is in a slump.

B : Brace yourself for unemployment.

A : 哦，天啊！股市下跌走空，經濟不景氣。

B : 做好失業的準備吧。

▶▶ bring sb. down 讓某人受挫

是要使某人遭受挫折而導致情緒低沉。

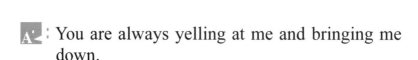

A : You are always yelling at me and bringing me down.

B : Well, if you would quit being so lazy, and get a job, then I wouldn't be yelling at you so much.

A : 你總是對我吼叫，會讓我受挫。

B : 嗯，如果你能改掉懶惰的壞毛病，而去找一份工作，那麼我將不會再對你吼叫了。

補充

yell at 對⋯吼叫。

▶▶ burst sb.'s bubble 刺破某人的幻想

解說

直譯「為刺破某人的泡泡」，就是讓某人希望破滅；bubble 幻想。

A : I hate to burst your bubble, but I overheard the managers talking, and you're not going to get the promotion.

B : You know something? I think I am just going to quit this stupid job.

A: 我真不想刺破你的幻想，但是我無意聽到經理們談話，你不會得到升遷。

B: 你聽說了什麼嗎？我想我正要辭掉這乏味的工作。

 ▶▶ **call off** 取消

解說

指活動、事件的取消。

A: I thought you were coming home for Christmas.

B: Several employees are sick, so the boss called off my leave.

A: 我以為你會回家過聖誕節。

B: 數個員工生病了，所以老闆取消我的休假。

補充

call off = cancel

▶▶ call the shots 做決定

解說

指負責拿主意或做決定。

: Why do you always let Steve call the shots?

B: It's because Steve is the boss's son, so we really have no say in the matter.

A: 你為什麼總是讓史蒂夫做決定呢?

B: 那是因為史蒂夫是老闆的兒子,所以我們在這件事情上真的沒有發言權。

補充

call the shots = make the decision;have no say in sth. 對某事沒有發言權。

▶▶ come straight from 直接來自

: I will come home straight from work tonight.

B: Why aren't you going to the gym, as usual?

A: 我今晚下班會直接回家。

B: 你為什麼不會像往常一樣去體育館呢?

▶▶ **come through** 解決問題

指身處困境或發生危險，而能安全度過難關，同時還有「到來」的意思，強調是必須經過數個程序才能完成，如 The innovation came through collaboration.（創新來自於合作。）

A : Can I rely on you to pick me up after work?

B : Of course. I always come through for you.

A : 下班後，我能靠你來接我嗎？

B : 當然可以，我一直都是幫你解決問題。

▶▶ **cut both ways** 互有利弊

指對雙方都起了作用，有利也有弊。

A : No wonder many people like the job because the pay is reasonable.

B : Well, it cuts both ways. To me, the hours are inconvenient.

：難怪許多人喜歡這工作，因為待遇很合理。

B：嗯，它互有利弊，對我來說，工作時間不方便。

▶▶ cut corners 走捷徑

解說

指用簡便辦法或省力方法來做事，其目的是為了節省時間或金錢，如 we cuts corners on every event.（我們用簡單方法來節省每一個活動的成本。）

A：We have to cut corners to get to where they are.

B：Sure, but some got there by breaking the law.

：我們必須走捷徑來趕上他們。

B：沒錯，但是有些人透過違法來達到目的。

補充

1. 常用句型為 Don't cut corners with health and safety.（為了健康與安全，不要走捷徑。）Don't take shortcuts.（不要走捷徑。）
2. get there 達到目的。

▶▶ draw a blank 突然忘記

直譯為「畫一個空白」，這裡指腦子一片空白，什麼都想不起來。

A : Who is on duty tonight?

B : I used to know, but now I'm drawing a blank.

A : 今晚誰值班？

B : 我曾經知道，但我現在突然忘記了。

▶▶ find out 發現

A : I just found out I get the promotion and raise.

B : Congratulations.

A : 我剛發現我得到升遷加薪。

B : 恭喜你。

聽到獲獎或得到好事情的回應句型 He deserve it. (他應得的。)

▶▶ for a living 維生

A : What do your parents do for a living?

B : My parents died when I was really young, and my grandparents raised me as their son.

A : 你父母是從事什麼工作維生？

B : 當我很年輕時，我的雙親就死了，而我的祖父母則把我當親生兒子撫養。

▶▶ for the sake of 為了

A : I'm going to work harder for the sake of my future.

B : I'm with you.

A : 為了將來，我要更努力工作。

B : 我支持你。

▶▶ from work 下班

A : Can you pick up a loaf of bread on the way home from work?

B : Sure, is there anything else we need?

> **A** : 你能在下班回家的路上買一條麵包嗎？
>
> **B** : 當然可以，我們還需要什麼呢？

pick up（買）用在隨意或偶然性的購買。

▶▶ get nothing on 沒有抓住把柄

A : Are you ready to get her fired?

B : We can't fire her. We've got nothing on her.

> **A** : 你準備解僱她嗎？
>
> **B** : 我們不能解僱她，我們沒有抓住她的把柄。

(補)(充)

get sth. on 抓住把柄。

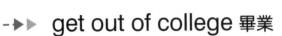

get out of college 畢業

A : What will you do after you get out of college?

B : Maybe I'll work a few years and then go to graduate school.

> **A** : 畢業後，你打算做什麼？
>
> **B** : 或許我會工作幾年，接著再去讀研究所。

give sb. a lift 讓某人搭便車

A : Can you give me a lift after work?

B : Sure, no problem.

> **A** : 下班後你能讓我搭便車嗎？
>
> **B** : 當然可以，沒問題。

補充

give sb. a lift = give sb. a ride; want a ride（想要搭便車）。

▶▶ go back to 回去

重新開始或返回到某種情境。

A: I'm thinking about going back to school.

B: That's a real good idea. Once you have a degree, many opportunities will present themselves.

A: 我正在考慮回去學校。

B: 那真是一個好主意，一旦你有了學位，許多機會會自己來。

▶▶ hard life 艱苦的生活

A: I don't want to live a hard life, which is why I am going to school.

B: A college education will definitely make many opportunities available.

A: 我不想要過艱苦的生活，那是我為什麼上學的原因。

B: 大學教育一定會創造許多機會。

▶▶ have sth. to do with 與某事有點關係

A : I cannot believe they actually hired me.

B : I guess that it has something to do with your expertise.

A : 我不敢相信他們真的錄用我。

B : 我猜想，這跟你的專長多少有點關係。

▶▶ in a tight spot 處於困境

指處於困難、困境與險惡之中。

A : I'm in a bit of a tight spot. Do you think you can loan me some money until I get paid?

B : Well, how much do you need?

A : 我手頭有點緊，你想你可以借我一些錢，等我發了工資再還給你嗎？

B : 嗯，你需要多少錢呢？

in a tight spot = in a tough spot

▶▶ **in every respect** 各方面

指在每一個方面。

A : I saw the notice that Mary got a raise.

B : She deserves it in every respect.

A : 我看見公告，瑪麗得到加薪。
B : 從各方面來看，她值得擁有。

in every respect = in all respects

▶▶ **in terms of** 就…而言

一般翻譯為「就…而論」、「在…方面」、「就…而言」。

A : What do you think of the manager, Michael?

B : In terms of character, he is a very down-to-earth person; but not in terms of management.

A : 你認為麥克經理怎麼樣？

B : 就個性而言，他是一個腳踏實地的人，但就管理而言，就不然了。

(補)(充)

down-to-earth 腳踏實地的。

▶▶ **invest in** 買／投資

(解)(說)

指買有用的東西，讓你做事更有效率或者可獲得一些好處。

A : Would you like to invest in some penny stocks?

B : It is a pity that I don't have any spare cash.

A : 你想要買進一些低價股嗎？

B : 可惜我沒有多餘的現金。

▶▶ just get over here 來我這裡

A: I have some things to take care of after work.

B: Just get over here as soon as you can. You don't want to miss the halftime show.

> **A:** 下班後，我有事情要處理。
> **B:** 盡快來我這裡，你不會想錯過中場秀表演。

補充
as soon as possible = as soon as you can 盡快。

▶▶ keep an eye on 照顧

解說
指留心或注意某人或某物，含有照顧的意思。

A: I'm going to Chicago on business next week. I need someone to keep an eye on my cat while I'm gone.

B: I'd like to, but I'll be away, too.

A: 下週我要去芝加哥出差,當我不在時,需要有人照顧我的貓。

B: 我很樂意,但是我也不在。

補充

1. keep an eye on = watchover
2. I'm gone. 口語中有兩種解釋,第一種是「我去世了」的意思,是死亡的婉約表示;另外一種是「我走了」的意思。

▶▶ **keep in touch with** 聯繫

解說

指保持聯繫。

A: Please see to it that you have to keep in touch with your boss on Mondays. You have to report the progress of work to him.

B: Thank you for reminding me. I'll go to his office.

A: 請注意,每個星期一你必須跟你的老闆聯繫,你必須跟他報告工作進度。

B: 謝謝你提醒我,我會去他的辦公室。

▶▶ keep track of 了解

指動態上的了解。

A : I'm trying to get adjusted to my new job. I think I can keep track of everything around here as soon as possible.

B : That's for sure. I think you are clever enough to catch up with your co-worker.

A : 我正在努力適應我的新工作,我想我能盡快了解到這裡每一件事情。

B : 那是肯定的,我想你夠聰明足夠跟上你的同事進度。

get adjusted 熟悉;catch up with 迎頭趕上。

▶▶ lay off 解僱

常指被裁員或被停止某項工作,其他類似說法有 You are fired. (你被炒魷魚了。)

PART

A : Did you hear that Ron was laid off?

B : Yeah, he was very unhappy because he worked for that company for over 20 years.

A : 你有聽說羅恩被解僱了嗎？

B : 有啊，他很不高興，因為他為那家公司工作超過了20年。

▶▶ let sb. down 讓某人失望

A : Why don't you just move to Hawaii and become a landscaper?

B : My parents really want me to go to college and get a degree, and I mustn't let them down.

A : 你為什麼不搬到夏威夷，且成為一位庭園設計家呢？

B : 我的父母親很想要我上大學讀書，取得學士學位，而我不能讓他們失望。

常用句型 I'm disappointed in you.（我對你失望。）

▶▶ miss out on 錯過

A: I like my job, and think I'll stick around after college.

B: Have you lost your mind? You would miss out on more options and more opportunities in your career.

A: 我喜歡我的工作，而且我想大學畢業後，我會繼續留下來。

B: 你瘋了嗎？你會在你的職業生涯中錯過更多的選擇與機會。

▶▶ next to none 最棒

A: I think Betty is good at English.

B: She's ok, but she's next to none in French.

A: 我覺得貝蒂的英語很好。

B: 她還好啦，但她在法語上才是最棒的。

▶▶ nominate sb. for sth.

提名某人為某事的候選人

A: If I nominate you for the technical advisor, will you accept it?

B: It would be an honor.

A: 如果我提名你為技術顧問候選人，你願意接受嗎？

B: 那將是一種榮幸。

▶▶ none the less 仍然

A: The show was entertaining, but none the less I'd rather have watched the season finale of Friends.

B: Well, thankfully, I recorded it.

A: 這節目有趣，但我仍然寧願看六人行本季的最後一集。

B: 嗯，幸好，我有錄下來。

not to mention 更不必說

 : Angel is good-looking and clever, not to mention being a good singer.

 : I think she is more like a star than a singer.

 : 安琪兒漂亮聰明，更不用說是一名好歌手。
 : 我想她比較像明星而不像歌手。

nothing short of 簡直是

解說

指強調接近於完全相同。

 : Bruce is nothing short of a genius.

 : I know. I cannot believe how smart that guy is.

 : 布魯斯簡直是一位天才。
 : 我知道，我不敢相信那傢伙是這麼聰明。

▶▶ pass for 被誤認為是

指被當作某人或某物。

A: Mary often passes for a celebrity.

B: I also often mistake her for a movie star.

A: 瑪麗常常被誤認為是社會名流。

B: 我也常常把她錯認為是電影明星。

▶▶ put sb. in charge 讓某人負責

A: I regret that I put him in charge.

B: You should have known that he was a slacker.

A: 我後悔讓他負責。

B: 你應該早就知道他是一位懶蟲。

▶▶ right down sb.'s alley
某人拿手的工作

直譯爲「恰是某人的路」。

A: Do you know anything about electronic repair?

B: That's right down my alley.

A: 你懂電器維修嗎？

B: 那正是我拿手的工作。

right down sb.'s alley = right up sb.'s alley; know anything about 懂／了解。

▶▶ save sb.'s breath 省點力氣

直譯爲「拯救某人的氣息」，是強調不要把時間、金錢或精力用在無用的請求或努力上。

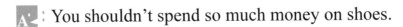

A: You shouldn't spend so much money on shoes.

B: You might as well save your breath. I've already made up my mind.

A：你不該花那麼多錢買鞋子。

B：你不妨省點力氣，我已經下定決心了。

補充

might as well 不妨 / 倒不如。

▶▶ **stay out of sth.** 不插手 / 別管 / 不干涉

解說

指置身於事情之外，保持不參與的態度。

A: Why won't you apologize to Jane?

B: You need to stay out of it, please.

A：你為什麼沒向珍道歉呢？

B：拜託，你別管此事。

▶▶ take off 請假

🅐: What can I do for you?

🅑: I'd like to take the day off and rest.

> 🅐: 我能幫忙你什麼嗎？
> 🅑: 我想要請假休息。

be on leave 休假中，on holiday = on vacation 度假，ask for leave 請假。

▶▶ take over 接管

🅐: My boss agreed that I'm going to take over the branch next week.

🅑: Congratulations.

> 🅐: 我老闆同意我下週接管這家分店。
> 🅑: 恭喜你。

▶▶ # take the words out of sb.'s mouth
先說出了某人要說的話

指說出某人的心裡話。

A: Despite years of study, I still cannot find a job.

B: You took the words right out of my mouth.

A: 儘管念書多年,我還不能找到一份工作。
B: 你先說出了我要說的話。

▶▶ # talk sb. out of sth.
說服某人不要做某事

A: Can you talk him out of leaving his job?

B: No, he is very set in his ways.

A: 你能說服他不要離職嗎?
B: 不能,他很固執於自己的方式。

▶▶ think twice 仔細考慮

指仔細衡量某事或某件東西。

A: Did you accept the position with Microsoft?

B: They provided me with such a great offer, that I didn't even need to think twice.

A: 你有接受微軟的職位嗎？

B: 他們提供我如此優厚的待遇，以致於我甚至不需要仔細考慮。

▶▶ wet behind the ears 嫩了點

指年輕毫無經驗與幼稚無知。

A: I think I should promote John to the local manager.

B: I feel he is too wet behind the ears to play such an important role.

A : 我想我應該提升湯姆為區域經理。

B : 我覺得他太嫩了點,還不能擔任如此重要角色。

▶▶ white lie 白色謊言

指無惡意的謊言。

A : You shouldn't lie about anything.

B : It was just a white lie, to make her feel good about herself, nothing serious.

A : 你不應該撒任何謊。

B : 這只是一個白色謊言,是為了讓她自主感覺良好,沒什麼要緊的。

▶▶ work overtime 加班

A : Who should we get to work overtime tonight?

B : It is Robert's turn.

：今晚我們誰應該加班呢？

 ：輪到羅伯特。

補充

常用句型 Do you get paid overtime?（你有拿到加班費了嗎？）
Why don't you leave it tomorrow?（你為什麼不明天做呢？）

(三) 辦公室瑣事

▶▶ **at the moment 目前**

解說

強調是此刻。

 ：Can you tell me what to do?

 ：At the moment, there is really nothing I can do.

 ：你能告訴我該怎麼辦呢？

 ：目前，我真的無能為力。

PART

▶▶ air conditioner 冷氣機

A: Be careful. The floor is slippery.

B: The air conditioner is leaking again, I guess.

A: 小心，地板很滑。

B: 我猜冷氣機又在漏水。

▶▶ belong to 屬於

A: Could I borrow the calculator?

B: I'm sorry. It doesn't belong to me.

A: 我能借用這臺計算機嗎？

B: 很抱歉，它不屬於我的。

 補充

借東西常用句型 Could I borrow...（我能借…？）、May I use...?（我能使用…？）Could you lend me your...?（你能把你的…借給我用嗎？）

PART

▶▶ beat around the bush 說話繞圈子

A : Tell me straight out; don't beat around the bush.

B : I don't like my boss.

> **A** : 直接說，不要說話繞圈子。
> **B** : 我不喜歡我的老闆。

▶▶ between ourselves 你我之間的祕密

A : I need to tell you something, but it is between ourselves.

B : Sure, what are friends for?

> **A** : 我必須告訴你一件事，但是它是你我之間的祕密。
> **B** : 當然，不然朋友是當假的嗎？

補充

between ourselves = between you and me.

149

▶▶ break into 闖入

解 說

用強制的手段進去。

A：Someone broke into my office last night and stole my computer.

B：Did the police come over and dust for fingerprints?

A：昨晚有人闖入我的辦公室，偷走我的電腦。

B：警察有過來採集指紋嗎？

▶▶ bury the hatchet 盡釋前嫌

A：Sorry, Mike. I often spoke badly of you in the past. Could you forgive me?

B：Let's bury the hatchet and be good friends again.

A：對不起，麥可，我以前常常說你壞話，你可以原諒我嗎？

B：讓我們盡釋前嫌，重新做好朋友吧。

▶▶ catch you later 等會兒見

A: I've got to head for work right now, so I'll catch you later.

B: Ok. Try to call me after work.

A: 我現在得去工作，所以等會兒見。

B: 好的，你下班後，要打電話給我。

catch you later = see you later

▶▶ come off as annoying 惹人討厭

A: I don't think I really like your friend David.

B: I know he can come off as annoying at first, but once you get to know him, he's a really cool guy.

A: 我想我真的不喜歡你的朋友大衛。

B: 我知道他一開始惹人討厭，但是一旦你認識他，他是個很不錯的人。

come off as + adj.（有著…的感覺）= give the impression as + adj.

▶▶ ## get sth. off sb.'s chest
把心中的話講出來

指發洩被壓抑的情緒、壓力或情感，而說出心裡話。

A: I need to get something off my chest.

B: Don't worry. I can keep a secret.

A: 我需要把心中的話講出來。

B: 不要擔心，我可以保守祕密。

▶▶ ## get out 洩漏

指消息或訊息的洩漏。

A : What I'm about to tell you, you can never let get out.

B : You can trust, that I won't tell a soul.

A : 我告訴你的事，你絕不能洩漏出去。

B : 你可以相信我，我不會告訴任何人。

補充

Get out the news or gossip.（傳出消息或謠言。）

▶▶ in person 親自

A : What is it that you want to talk to me about?

B : I'd rather talk about this in person. Can you meet me at the office?

A : 你想要跟我討論什麼呢？

B : 我較喜歡親自討論，你能來辦公室見我嗎？

▶▶ lock up 鎖上

A : I have to visit my client now.

B : Do you want me to lock up the door before I leave?

A : 我現在必須去拜訪我的客戶。

B : 你要我離開之前鎖門嗎？

▶▶ make a point of 一定

解說

一般翻譯為「重視」或「強調」，含有一定要做的意思。

A : I can't believe my electric bill this month was so high.

B : Well, that happened to me once, so now I make a point of turning off all the lights before I leave the house.

A : 我無法相信我這個月的電費這麼高了。

B : 嗯，這種事情我以前也發生過，所以現在離開房子之前，我一定會關掉所有的燈。

▶▶ make an appointment 預約時間

A : May I make an appointment with you?

B : Sure. Please make an appointment with my secretary.

A : 我可以跟你預約時間見面嗎？

B : 可以，請跟我的祕書預約時間見面。

▶▶ run out of 用完

指補充品的用完。

A : The printer ran out of ink. Where do I find the new ink cartridge?

B : I think it is in the storeroom.

A : 印表機用完了墨水，我從哪裡可以找到新的墨水匣呢？

B : 我想它在儲藏室裡。

▶▶ speak ill of 說壞話

A: I have the feeling that Marcy often speaks ill of me behind my back.

B: I heard she likes you, and she is just asking people how she should approach you.

A: 我有一種感覺，瑪西常在背後說我的壞話。

B: 我聽說她喜歡你，她只是問別人她應該如何接近你。

▶▶ stay put 停在原地

A: I'm new here. I can't find your office.

B: Just stay put, all right? I pick you up right now.

Ａ：我對這裡不熟，我找不到你的辦公室。

Ｂ：停在原地，好嗎？我現在立刻去接你。

▶▶ think straight 頭腦清醒

Ａ：I wasn't thinking straight when I told you that I didn't want to be your friend anymore.

Ｂ：Don't even sweat it. I consider it never happened.

Ａ：當我告訴你，我不想再當你的朋友時，我的頭腦並不清醒。

Ｂ：別擔心，我會當作那從來沒有發生過。

補充

sweat it 有「流汗」或「為此擔心」意思。

(四) 公司

 ## a whole new ball game
一種全新的局面

解說

ball game 局面，ball game = situation。

A: Since the evolution of the internet, operating a business has become a whole new ball game.

B: No doubt. The need for Online Marketing expertise is increasing, and the number of competitors has jumped sky high.

A: 自從網路革命以後，經營事業變成一種全新的局面。

B: 難怪，網路行銷知識需求逐漸增加，而競爭者的數目暴增。

at the age of 在…幾歲的時候

A: Your son is really something.

B: Yes, he is. He started his own company at the age of 20.

：你的兒子真的很了不起。

：對，沒錯，他在20歲的時候創辦了自己的公司。

補充

start his company 創辦他的公司，run his company 經營他的公司。

▶▶ be torn between 難於抉擇

解說

指左右為難或難於抉擇，造成無法選擇。

：Which company do you want to go to?

：I'm torn between Sony Company and Samsung Company.

：你想去哪間公司呢？（這裡的 which 可以用 what 代替）

：我在索尼公司與三星公司之間難於抉擇。

1

PART

▶▶ **change sb.'s mind** 改變某人的主意

A: I heard your company is going to hire a new sales person next month.

B: Yes, but now the boss has changed his mind.

> **A:** 我聽說你們公司下個月要聘用一位新的銷售人員。
>
> **B:** 沒錯,但是現在老闆已經改變他的主意了。

▶▶ **get off the ground** 順利起步

指活動或事業一開始就很順利。

A: Without your help, the company would never get off the ground.

B: You're welcome. It's my pleasure.

> **A:** 沒有你的幫忙,這公司就無法開始起步。
>
> **B:** 別客氣,這是我的榮幸。

160

▶▶ go out of business 停業

指停業、破產或倒閉。

A：The company you worked for went out of business.

B：That's because there is too much competition in the market.

A：你以前工作的公司停業了。

B：那是因為市場上有太多的競爭。

▶▶ have a hunch 有預感

A：I have a hunch that my business is going to do well.

B：That would be awesome.

A：我有預感，我的公司會經營的很好。

B：那太棒了。

PART

I have an intuition that... 我直覺…

▶▶ fall on difficult times 陷入經濟困境

是指經濟出現問題；fall on 落到。

A: After investment losses, the company fell on difficult times.

B: Yeah, but now it is beginning to get back in shape.

A: 這家公司投資失利後，就陷入經濟困境。

B: 沒錯，但是現在這家公司正開始恢復到原來的狀況。

1. fall on difficult times = fall on hard times
2. get back in shape 恢復身材，用到公司情境指恢復原狀。

▶▶ have enough brains to do sth.

有足夠的頭腦去做某事

形容夠聰明。

A : I was rejected by every company.

B : You should've known you don't have enough brains to get into these companies.

A : 我被每一間公司拒絕。

B : 你早該知道，你沒有足夠的才智進入這些公司。

reject（拒絕）= refuse = turn down = decline（婉轉的拒絕必須用此單字）

▶▶ roll out the red carpet 盛大歡迎

鋪上紅色地毯，表示盛大歡迎；roll out 鋪開。

A : We are ready to roll out the red carpet to British investors.

B : Is everything ready?

A : 我們準備盛大歡迎英國投資者。

B : 一切都準備好了嗎？

▶▶ **stop...with** 停止與

A : I am about to stop doing business with you.

B : I'm very sorry, Sir. Can you tell me what the problem is?

A : 我要停止與你做生意。

B : 先生，很抱歉，你可以告訴我是什麼問題嗎？

What's the problem?（出了什麼事呢？）= What's wrong? = What's the matter?

▶▶ wind up 結束

指停止活動。

A : How about winding up the company?

B : I believe it's not too difficult to do.

> **A** : 結束公司營業,你看怎麼樣?
>
> **B** : 我相信結束營業並不太難。

(補)(充)
wind up = finish up

(五) 科技

▶▶ acquire a taste 開始喜歡

強調對某事感到有興趣或喜歡。

A : I can't make sense out of the website.

B : I think I haven't acquired a taste for the shop online yet.

PART

A : 我看不懂這個網站。

B : 我想我還沒開始喜歡線上購物。

 cutting edge 先進的

A : Have you heard about nanotechnology?

B : I heard it's supposed to be real cutting edge stuff.

A : 你有聽說過奈米技術嗎？

B : 我聽說它應該是很先進的東西。

補充

real 非常。

 eye-opening 很有啟發性的

解說

直譯爲「大開眼界」，引申爲「很有啟發性的」。

A : Looks like it's going to be an interesting and eye-opening finding.

B : I hope so. I put a lot of hours into it.

A : 看起來像是一個有趣且很有啓發性的發現。

B : 我希望如此，我投入了很多時間在裡面。

▶▶ **get lost** 迷失

指迷路不見。

A : Some of my email is missing. How did that happen?

B : It does not happen often, but sometimes my emails have gotten lost in cyber space.

A : 我的電子郵件有些不見了，怎麼會這樣呢？

B : 它沒有常常發生，但是有時候我的電子郵件會迷失在網際網路空間中。

▶▶ get the hang of sth. 學會某物

指很清楚掌握住某物的用法與訣竅。

A: I can't operate the computer very well.

B: Don't worry. If you practice it every day, you'll get the hang of it soon.

A: 我不能熟練地使用電腦。

B: 不要擔心,如果你每天練習,你很快就會學會使用電腦。

▶▶ give it a go 試一試

A: Do you think you can help me fix my computer?

B: Well, I'm not a computer maintenance engineer, but I'll give it a go.

A: 你想你可以幫我修理電腦嗎?

B: 嗯,我不是一位電腦維修工程師,但是我會試一試。

補充

give it a go = give it a try

▶▶ ## have nothing to do with sth.
跟某事無關

A: I don't care what I do for a living, just as long as it has nothing to do with computers.

B: Well, then you're not going to have that many choices.

A: 我不在乎我是做什麼維生,只要跟電腦無關就好。

B: 嗯,那麼你將不會有太多的選擇。

▶▶ ## No sweat. 沒關係 / 不用擔心

A: I'd like to verify my account using Facebook but the password doesn't seem to work.

B: No sweat. I can issue you a new password.

A: 我想要確認我臉書上的帳號,但是密碼似乎不管用。

B: 沒關係,我可以給你發一份新的密碼。

 補 充

No sweat. = It doesn't matter. = Never mind.

▶▶ state-of-the-art 尖端技術

 解 說

強調某物用最新技術和方法製作而成,已發展出相當程度的技術水準。

A : Scientists use state-of-the-art technology to prove their theories.

B : Some of the stuff they come up with is amazing.

A : 科學家使用尖端技術來證明他們的理論。

B : 他們提出的一些東西真是了不起。

第 **2** 單元

PART

職場生活場景片語

01 人際關係
（幫助用語、聯絡用語、拒絕、拜訪、陪伴、好心、募捐、祕密）

02 金錢場景
（有錢、缺錢、花錢、賺錢）

03 健康場景
（身體好、疾病、生病症狀、生病治療）

04 情緒場景
（心情好、心情不好、生氣、緊張、放鬆）

05 時間場景
（慢、快、開始、結束）

06 購物消費
（便宜、很貴、免費、其他）

01 人際關係

(一) 幫助用語

▶▶ **at sb.'s service** 隨時提供服務

A : Could you give me a hand with my bag?

B : Sure. I'm at your service.

A : 你能幫我拿我的手提包嗎？

B : 當然可以，我隨時為你提供服務。

▶▶ **fall back on** 求助於（轉而依靠）

A : I've had to fall back on my family for financial help since I lost my job.

B : That sounds like you are in trouble.

A : 自從我失業後，我必須依靠家裡的經濟援助。

B : 聽起來你好像遇到了困難。

▶▶ give sb. a hand 幫忙某人

A : Would you give me a hand, please? I have a paper due on Monday.

B : I'd like to, but I'm afraid I don't have any spare time.

> **A** : 請你幫我個忙，好嗎？我有份報告星期一要交出。
>
> **B** : 我很樂意，但恐怕我抽不出任何時間。

補 充

當幫忙以此型式 give sb. a big hand 來表達時，此片語又可解釋為「為某人鼓掌」。

▶▶ do sb. a favor 幫忙某人

A : Would you do me a favor and pick the kids up from school for me?

B : Sure, no problem.

> **A** : 你能幫我去學校接小孩嗎？
>
> **B** : 當然可以，沒問題。

do sb. a favor = give sb. a hand = give sb. a favor；在英文中的 do 可用來替代任何動詞，若動詞忘了不會說，就用 do 就對了，但用 do 替代別的動詞，有一缺點就是表達不夠明確，會讓聽到者猜測 do 是代表什麼意思。

▶▶ **help out 幫助**

用在幫助某人解決問題或度過難關。

A : Why are you going back home this weekend?

B : My family and I are going to help out at the local volunteer center.

A : 這個週末你為什麼要回家？

B : 我的家人和我要去當地的義工中心幫忙。

補充

常用句型為 How can I help out?（我能幫你做點什麼嗎？）

174

PART

(二) 聯絡用語

▶▶ **drop sb. a line** 寫封短信給某人

line 是指短信或便條的意思。

A: I haven't heard from Sally for a long time. I wonder how she's doing now.

B: Well, I'll give you her e-mail address if you want to drop her a line.

A: 我好久沒有莎莉的消息了,我想知道她現在怎麼樣。

B: 嗯,如果你要寫信給她,我會給你她的電子郵件地址。

常用句型為 Do you have questions or comments? Drop me a line I would love to hear from you.(你有任何的問題或意見?寫信給我,我很喜歡收到你的來信。)

▶▶ get in touch with sb. 與某人取得聯繫

 解說

get in 有進入的意思，這裡的 touch 是聯繫的意思。

A : Did you get in touch with your ex-girlfriend?

B : Yes, we were happy to be together.

A : 你有跟你的前任女朋友聯繫嗎？

B : 有啊，我們很高興在一起。

補充

be together（在一起），get together（聚在一起）。

▶▶ get through to 聯絡

 解說

get through 有到達的意思，而 get through to 強調是否有成功地和某人聯繫。

A : Did you get through to the customer complaints department?

B : No, the line was busy.

A： 你有聯絡顧客投訴部門嗎？

B： 沒有，這支電話一直占線中。

▶▶ hear from sb. 接到某人的信

A： Have you kept in touch with Amy after she went abroad?

B： I hear from her once a month.

A： 在艾咪出國後，你有跟她保持聯絡嗎？

B： 我每個月都有收到她一次的來信。

▶▶ in touch with sb. 與某人有聯繫

指處在於某種狀態下的聯繫。

A： Are you still in touch with anyone from university?

B： No, we all kind of lost touch.

A：你大學畢業後，還有跟同學聯繫嗎？

B：沒有，我們都有點失去聯繫了。

▶▶ touch base with sb. 與某人有聯繫

A：Do you still touch base with John?

B：Sorry, we've been out of touch for ages.

A：你還有跟約翰聯絡嗎？

B：抱歉，我們已經好久沒聯絡了。

(三) 拒絕

▶▶ put down 放下

A：That's a pretty good book. I simply couldn't put it down.

B：Cool, I'll have to read it sometime myself.

A：那是一本相當好的書，我簡直捨不得把它放下來。

B：酷啊，我得找時間親自閱讀它。

put down 有「寫下」的意思，如 I put my name down on the waiting list for next course. 我在下一個課程等候名單上，寫下我的名字。

▶▶ turn a deaf ear to 拒絕聽

用在忽視某人說的話。

A : Did you apologize to her?

B : I sure did. I tried to explain it, but she turned a deaf ear to my excuses.

A : 你有向她道歉了嗎？

B : 當然有，我想要解釋，但是她拒絕聽我的理由。

▶▶ turn down 拒絕

指拒絕某件事情，或者是拒絕某人的建議或忠告等等。

A: I heard you turned down the job in the end.

B: Yes, it really wasn't what I was looking for.

A: 我聽說你最後拒絕了這份工作。

B: 沒錯，它真的不是我想找的。

找工作相關片語 apply for a job（申請一份工作）job hunting（找工作）morning shift（早班）night shift（晚班）recruit employees online（線上招募員工）

▶▶ turn sb.'s back on 拒絕

A: You always turn your back on me when I ask you to lend me some money.

B: It's because you never pay back loans.

A: 當我要求你借我一些錢時，你總是拒絕我。

B: 那是因為你欠錢不還。

(四) 拜訪

drop by 拜訪

解說

指停下做短時間的拜訪。

A: I've not seen Helen for ages.

B: She said that she might drop by my place to-night. Will you come over?

A: 我已經好久沒見到海倫了。

B: 她說她今晚會來拜訪我，你要過來嗎？

補充

1. drop by = drop at = drop in = drop over
2. 邀請常用句型 Do you want to come over / along? / Care to join us?

look up 拜訪

A: I should look my uncle up on the way home.

B: Good idea. He'd be pleased to see you, I'm sure.

PART

A： 在回家路上我應該拜訪我的舅舅。

B： 好主意，我相信他會很高興見到你。

look up = look in

▶▶ stop by 順便訪問

A： I'll stop by the drugstore to pick up my prescription on my way home.

B： Could you pick up some diet cokes for me?

A： 在回家路上，我會順便去藥房取我的藥方。

B： 你能順便幫我買低糖可樂嗎？

其他拜訪片語 stop in = stop over = stop by；call at somewhere = call round somewhere；pay a visit to = make a call to = pay a call to

(五) 陪伴

▶▶ **accompany sb. to sth.** 伴隨某人去

accompany 是陪伴的意思。

A : I've never seen Amy before. Would you care to accompany me to meet her at the airport?

B : Sure. I've met her once or twice before.

A : 我從來沒兒過艾咪，你願意陪我去機場接她嗎？

B : 當然可以，我以前見過她一兩次。

常用句型為 Would you care to...? = Would you like to...? （你想…？）

▶▶ **keep sb. company** 陪伴某人

A : Ever since Amy bought a kitty to keep her company, I've not been to her home.

B : I almost forgot you have an allergy to cats.

A: 自從艾咪買了一隻小貓來陪伴她，我就沒有去過她家。

B: 我都快忘了，你對貓過敏。

▶▶ **walk sb. home** 陪某人走路回家

A: May I walk you home?

B: Thanks a lot. But Vincent will give me a lift home.

A: 我能陪你走路回家嗎？

B: 謝謝，但是文森會讓我搭便車回家。

(補)(充)

drive sb. home 開車送某人回家，see sb. home 送某人回家。

(六) 好心

▶▶ **a heart of gold** 心地好

(解)(說)

gold 一般被認為是具有極大價值或美德的東西，a heart of gold 為一顆黃金般的心，引申為心地很好。

184

A: Rachel is a clever lady with a heart of gold.

B: Yeah, she is so kind-hearted.

A: 瑞秋是心地好的聰明淑女。

B: 是啊，她心地很好。

▶▶ have a heart 發發慈悲

指發發慈悲或發揮同情心；這裡的 heart 是指憐憫或同情的能力。

A: Have a heart. I'm tired. Could you give me a lift?

B: I have no room in my car. You could try Andy.

A: 發發慈悲，我累了，你能讓我搭便車嗎？

B: 我的車子沒位置了，你可以去問一下安迪。

很累常用句型 I'm tired (out). / I'm beat. / I'm exhausted. / I'm burned out. / I'm out of stream.

▶▶ one in a million 大好人

A : It was good of John to give me a hand with my assignment.

B : Yes, he's definitely one in a million.

A : 約翰真好，幫忙我的作業。

B : 對啊，他的確是大好人。

(七) 募捐

▶▶ chip in 捐助

用在捐錢或出力。

A : It is reported that many people are homeless after the earthquake.

B : Let's chip in some money to help them.

A : 報導說，地震過後，有許多人變成無家可歸。

B : 我們捐助一些錢來幫助他們吧。

▶▶ make a contribution to 捐助

contribution 指捐錢或出力的行為。

A: Our club decided to raise some funds to make a contribution to the poor.

B: It's a good thing. Please count me in.

> **A:** 我們社團決定募集資金來捐助貧窮的人。
>
> **B:** 它是好事,請把我算上。

▶▶ pass the hat round 募捐／集資／籌款

以前美國教堂在做禮拜結束前,都會拿一頂帽子出來,希望信徒捐錢蓋教堂,後來引申到大家捐錢為朋友解決困難。

A: Betty's birthday is coming up. I don't have enough money to buy her a nice present.

B: Then I think we should pass the hat round and share it.

A: 貝蒂的生日快到了,我沒有足夠的錢買給她一份好的禮物。

B: 那麼我想我們應該募捐來分擔費用。

▶▶ take up a collection for 為…募捐

take up 是開始從事;collection 是指捐款。

A: I heard the school took up a collection for building the new dormitory.

B: Well, I'd like to donate some money for it.

A: 我聽說學校為建新宿舍募捐。

B: 嗯,我想要為它捐獻一些錢。

(八) 祕密

▶▶ between you and me
我們之間的祕密

 : If I tell you a personal thing, it's between you and me.

 : I promise I'll keep your secret.

> **A** : 如果我告訴你一個私人的事，它是我們之間的祕密。
>
> **B** : 我保證我會保守祕密。

補充

between you and me = keep between the two of us.

▶▶ let the cat out of the bag
無意間祕密洩露

解說

把貓從袋裡放出來，就是洩露祕密。

A : We'll throw a surprise party for Mary to cel-ebrate her birthday this Sunday.

B : Unfortunately, John let the cat out of the bag and told her.

A : 我們在這個星期日會為瑪麗舉辦驚喜宴會來慶祝她的生日。

B : 不幸的是，約翰無意間將祕密洩露給她知道了。

▶▶ keep a secret 保守祕密

A : Can you keep a secret?

B : You can trust I won't tell anyone.

A : 你可以保守祕密嗎？
B : 你可以相信我不會告訴任何人。

▶▶ keep it to oneself 保密

A : When it comes to personal matters, I prefer to keep it to myself.

B : Don't worry. I'll keep it a secret.

A: 當談到個人的事情，我較喜歡保密。

B: 不要擔心，我會保守祕密。

▶▶ tell a soul 告訴任何人

soul 本來是靈魂、精神的意思，在一些歌詞中出現的 soul 是指稱人，而這裡的 a soul 等於 anyone。

A: I want to share with you a secret.

B: I won't tell a soul.

A: 我想要與你分享一個祕密。

B: 我不會告訴任何人。

▶▶ trade secret 商業祕密

A: Bill Gates has many trade secrets in the software industry.

B: I suppose that is how he became so wealthy.

A：比爾蓋茲在軟體工業有許多商業祕密。

B：我想那是他致富的方法。

「保守祕密」的其他說法：keep sth. secret from sb.，zip sb.'s mouth。

 金錢場景

(一) 有錢

 an arm and a leg 許多錢

解說

指任何東西要你付出一隻手臂和一隻腳,表示東西很貴,要花很多錢。

A : Did you see Bill's new jacket?

B : Yeah, it must cost him an arm and a leg.

A : 你有看到比爾的新夾克嗎?

B : 有,它一定花掉他許多錢。

 be born with a silver spoon in sb.'s mouth 出生富貴

解說

be born with 生而俱有,silver spoon 財富。

A : She was born with a silver spoon in her mouth.

B : Yes. She was spending money like water.

A : 她出生富貴之家。

B : 沒錯,她花錢像流水一樣。

 be loaded 很有錢

A : I bought a watch yesterday.

B : You bought another one. You're loaded.

A : 我昨天買一只手錶。

B : 你又買了另一只手錶,你很有錢啊。

be made of money 很有錢

解說

是錢做成的,表示錢很多。

A : Do you want to take a trip with us? It will cost about 200 dollars per person.

B : Do you think I'm made of money?

：你要跟我們去旅行嗎？每人將花費約200元。

：你認為我很有錢嗎？

▶▶ come into a fortune 繼承一筆遺產

：I have heard rumors that you have come into a fortune.

：Are you kidding? I can hardly afford to eat.

：我聽到謠言，說你繼承了一筆遺產。

：你開什麼玩笑？我幾乎沒錢用餐。

補充

come into a fortune = inherit a fortune.

▶▶ cost a pretty penny 一筆相當大的錢

解說

pretty 相當大，penny 一筆錢。

A: Did you see Helen wearing a sapphire bracelet?

B: I surely did. It must have cost a pretty penny.

A: 你有看到海倫戴著藍寶石手鐲嗎？

B: 我當然有，它一定很貴。

▶▶ deep pocket 經濟狀況很好

深口袋，表示經濟狀況良好；而 tight pocket 緊口袋，表示經濟不好。

A: I have a tight pocket. I'm short of 2,000 dollars for the new car.

B: Don't look at me. I don't have a deep pocket.

A: 我手頭很緊，我缺2,000美元買新車。

B: 不要指望我，我經濟狀況沒有很好。

▶▶ have money to burn 有用不完的錢

有錢要燒掉，表示錢多的用不完。

A : The coffee service is 100 bucks.

B : Do you think I'm Bill Gates, and have money to burn?

A : 這套咖啡器具是100元。

B : 你認為我是比爾蓋茲，有用不完的錢嗎？

▶▶ pretty penny 很多錢

A : He earned a pretty penny investing in the stock market.

B : I should ask him what to invest in.

A : 他投資股票市場賺了很多錢。

B : 我應該問他要投資什麼。

PART

賺很多錢的其他說法：roll in dough, wall in dough, rake in the dough。

(二) 缺錢

▶▶ **as poor as a church mouse** 很窮

解說
像教堂的老鼠一樣窮，就是很窮。

A: He is as poor as a church mouse since he went out of business.

B: I believe that will not always be the case.

A: 自從他破產後，就很窮。

B: 我相信情況不會永遠是這樣。

▶▶ **be flat broke** 很窮

指一個錢也沒有；flat 完全地。

A : I'm flat broke after the trip. I can't even afford a cup of coffee now.

B : Well. Vacations cost you a lot of money.

A : 在這次旅行過後,我就身無分文,我現在連一杯咖啡都買不起。

B : 喔,度假花掉了你很多錢。

be (flat) broke = clean broke = stone broke = stony broke

▶▶ **be hard up** 缺錢

A : I'm a bit hard up for cash because I want to buy a new car.

B : I can loan you some money, if you need help.

A : 我有點缺錢,因為我想買一輛新車。

B : 如果你需要幫忙,我可以借你一些錢。

▶▶ be poorly off 生活貧困

A: How much do you know about Vincent van Gogh?

B: He painted many great works even though he was so poorly off all his life.

> **A:** 你對這個梵谷了解多少呢？
>
> **B:** 雖然他一生生活貧困，但他畫出了許多偉大的作品。

▶▶ for a rainy day 以防不時之需

為雨天做準備，意思為未雨綢繆，以防不時之需。

A: I evaluated my finances recently.

B: Well. Do you have some money for a rainy day?

> **A:** 我最近評估了我的財務狀況。
>
> **B:** 嗯，你有存一些錢以防不時之需嗎？

▶▶ in debt 負債

A: I'm wondering if you could loan me some money.

B: I don't have money to lend. Going to a university has put me in debt.

A: 我想知道你是否能借我一些錢。

B: 我沒有錢可以借，上大學已經讓我負債了。

▶▶ in the hole 負債

A: I'm about two thousand dollars in the hole since I invested in the stock market.

B: Yes, but at least you look like a rich woman.

A: 自從投資股票市場，我大約負債2,000美元。

B: 沒錯，但是至少你看起來像一位有錢人。

▶▶ in the red 虧損

解說

red 赤字。

A : Is the company in the red?

B : No. The new marketing method has put the company in the positive.

A : 這家公司正在虧損嗎？

B : 不，新的行銷方法已經使得公司有起色了。

▶▶ go broke 破產

A : Many customers didn't shop there because of bad service.

B : So, it was no surprise to me when the company went broke.

A : 因為服務不好，許多消費者不在那裡購物。

B : 所以，當這間公司破產時，我並不感到吃驚。

▶▶ keep sb.'s head above water
不負債

A: I heard Jill fired five students.

B: She needs to cut labor costs to keep her head above water.

A: 我聽說吉兒解僱了5位學生。

B: 她需要削減勞工成本來使她不負債。

▶▶ live beyond sb.'s means 超支

A: The house rent may go up again.

B: No kidding. I don't want to live beyond my means.

A: 房租可能再上漲。

B: 不要開玩笑了,我不想要超支。

▶▶ make ends meet 量入為出

A: The newspaper said college students are made of money.

B: But it's hard for me to make ends meet as it is.

A: 報紙說，大學生很有錢。

B: 但是事實上，要維持收支平衡對我而言很困難。

▶▶ pinch and scrape 省吃儉用

A: I have to pinch and scrape to pay room and board.

B: I feel the same way. I don't have any spare money to buy clothes or anything.

A: 我必須省吃儉用來付食宿費。

B: 我有同感，我沒有任何閒錢來買衣服或其他東西。

補充

pinch and scrape = scrape and screw

▶▶ pinch pennies 精打細算

A: Many students have to pinch pennies to get through college.

B: Yes. The cost of going to school has gotten way too high.

> **A:** 許多學生必須精打細算來上大學。
>
> **B:** 是啊,上學的花費已經變太高了。

▶▶ tight budget 經濟拮据

A: I cannot afford nice restaurants. I'm on a tight budget.

B: Don't worry. I'll pick up the tab tonight.

> **A:** 我供應不起高級餐廳的開支,我經濟拮据。
>
> **B:** 不要擔心,今晚我來付帳。

補充

tight budget = tight pocketbook

PART

(三) 花錢

burn a hole in sb.'s pocket
荷包大失血

 解說

直譯為「口袋裡燒了一個洞」，指一有錢就不留，急於把錢花光。

A: Every week my car needs repairs.

B: I am sure it's starting to burn a hole in your pocket.

A: 每週我的車子都需要修理。
B: 我肯定你的荷包開始大失血。

dig into sb.'s pocket 掏腰包

 解說

指花錢。

A: Can you reduce your expenditures every month?

B: Of course not. I have to dig into my pocket to pay those expenses.

206

A : 你每月可以減少你的開支嗎？

B : 當然不可以，我必須掏腰包來付那些費用。

▶▶ pay the earth for 花很多錢

A : I paid the earth for the new car. I don't know if it's worth that much.

B : I don't think I'd pay that much.

A : 我花很多錢買這輛新車，我不知道是否值得那麼多錢。

B : 我想我不願意付那麼多錢。

▶▶ pay through the nose 花很多錢

A : I'm sure that the purse is genuine, so I'll pay through the nose for it.

B : To tell you the truth, it is a fake one.

A : 我確信這個皮包是真貨，所以我會花很多錢買它。

B : 告訴你實話，它是假貨。

▶▶ **spend money like water** 揮霍無度

指花錢如流水一樣。

A: Why don't you go shopping with us?

B: I feel like I'm a bit of shopping queen and spend money like water when I'm feeling low.

A: 你為什麼不跟我們去購物呢？

B: 在我心情低落時，我想我有點像是血拼女王，揮霍無度。

▶▶ **throw sb.'s money away** 亂花錢

A: Tim constantly throws his money away.

B: That's true. He often purchases things he does not need.

A: 提姆經常地亂花錢。

B: 這是真的，他常購買他不需要的東西。

(四) 賺錢

▶▶ be good money 有利可圖的投資

A: I heard there is good money in running a coffee shop.

B: You are so simple-minded that you actually believe that.

> **A:** 我聽說經營咖啡店很賺錢。
>
> **B:** 你是如此的頭腦簡單以致於真的相信。

▶▶ cash in on sth. 靠某物賺錢

A: Alaska uses its beautiful scenery to cash in on tourist dollars.

B: In other words, it is a very beautiful place to explore.

> **A:** 阿拉斯加州利用美麗的風景來賺觀光客的錢。
>
> **B:** 換句話說，它是一個探險的好地方。

▶▶ make a fortune 賺大錢

A : I wish I could be like Bill Gates and make a fortune.

B : So do I. We need to invent something clever and useful.

> **A** : 我希望我能像比爾蓋茲一樣賺大錢。
>
> **B** : 我也是，我們得發明靈巧有用的東西。

補充

make a fortune = make big money.

▶▶ make a killing 突然賺得一大筆錢

A : Do you know about the Buffet story?

B : He made a killing investing in the stock market.

> **A** : 你知道巴菲特的故事嗎？
>
> **B** : 他投資股票市場賺了一大筆錢。

▶▶ make ends meet 收支相抵

A: There are a few job openings at the mall.

B: I won't be able to make ends meet on the wages they pay.

A: 購物中心有一些職位空缺。

B: 靠他們發放的工資，我不能做到收支相抵。

make ends meet = make both ends meet；job opening = job vacancy 職位空缺。

▶▶ money grow on trees 賺錢很容易

錢長在樹上，喻賺錢是很容易。

A: Can I borrow some money from you?

B: Sorry, I can't lend you anything. Do you think money grows on trees?

A: 我能向你借一些錢嗎？

B: 抱歉，我不能借錢給你。你覺得賺錢很容易嗎？

03 健康場景

(一) 身體好

▶▶ **be in the picture of health** 很健康

A : You look to be in the picture of health.

B : I often take advantage of my spare time to exercise.

A : 你看起來很健康。

B : 我常利用空閒時間來做運動。

▶▶ **as fit as a fiddle** 身體很健康

用小提琴 (fiddle) 形容身體健康。

A : He is over eighty years old but is as fit as a fiddle.

B : I guess the exercise program is working.

A: 他超過80歲,但是他身體很健康。

B: 我想運動課程正起了作用。

▶▶ as right as rain 非常健康

強調身體恢復正常。

A: Hi, Helen. I heard you had an operation last month. How are you doing?

B: Actually, after the treatment, I'm as right as rain now.

A: 喂,海倫,我聽說妳上個月動手術,妳還好嗎?

B: 事實上,經過治療後,我現在非常健康。

▶▶ in good shape 身體健康

shape 身材。

A : You look like you are in very good condition. How do you keep in such good shape?

B : Well, combining exercise and diet is the good way to keep healthy.

A : 你看起來身體很健康，你如何保持身體如此健康呢？

B : 嗯，運動和飲食的結合是維持健康的有益方法。

補充

若 in good shape 的主詞是物，則其意義為「處於良好狀態」，如 The machine is in good shape. 這機器狀況良好。

▶▶ fresh as a daisy 精神飽滿的

解說

直譯為「像雛菊一樣新鮮」，形容精力充沛。

A : I feel as fresh as a daisy after a night of restful sleep.

B : You look like a million bucks.

：一夜安穩的睡眠後，我覺得精神飽滿。

B：你看來精力充沛。

▶▶ in fine feather 精神很好

直譯爲「有好的羽毛」，形容像鳥一樣精神飽滿。

A：I really feel in fine feather after taking a nap.

B：You bet. A good rest is good for your health.

A：在午睡後，我真的覺得精神很好。

B：你說的沒錯，好的休息有利於健康。

▶▶ keep fit 保持健康

fit 健康的。

A : How do you keep fit?

B : I keep myself in good shape by going for a walk every day.

A : 你如何保持身體健康呢?
B : 我每天散步來保持自己的身體健康。

(二) 疾病

▶▶ **act up** 復發

A : Oh, man. My allergies are acting up.

B : I think you are allergic to the pollen.

A : 哦,天啊,我的過敏復發了。
B : 我想你是對花粉過敏。

▶▶ **be allergic to** 對…過敏

A : My skin is itchy and dry. Could you tell me why?

B : It sounds like you are allergic to something.

A：我的皮膚很癢而且乾燥，你可以告訴我原因嗎？

B：聽起來好像你對某種東西過敏。

▶▶ **come down with** 染上

指染上或得了病。

A：I don't have much of an appetite. I feel like I came down with a cold.

B：I think you should call and make an appointment with a doctor.

A：我沒有什麼胃口，我想我染上了感冒。

B：我想你應該打電話跟醫生預約一個時間。

▶▶ **off color** 精神不好

A：You look off color as if you were ill. Wouldn't you be better off washing your face?

B：Thank you for your suggestion, but I don't want to go out.

217

PART

A: 你看起來精神不好，好像生病似的，你不覺得去洗臉一下會比較好嗎？

B: 謝謝你的建議，但我不想要出去。

 on the mend 在恢復健康中

解說

mend 好轉。

A: It's nice to have you back. I'm so glad to see you're on the mend.

B: Thanks a lot. I hope I can catch up on my work as soon as possible.

A: 很高興你回來了，我很高興看見你正在恢復健康中。

B: 謝謝，我希望能盡快把工作趕完。

 out of shape 身體不好

解說

指身體狀況不佳。

218

A : I'm told that John is so out of shape lately.

B : John needs to start watching what he eats and exercise regularly.

A : 我聽說約翰最近身體很不好。

B : 約翰需要開始注意飲食和定期做運動。

▶▶ **under the weather** 身體不舒服

人的心情會隨天氣而變化，尤其是在烏雲滿日的壞天氣下，人的心情就會憂鬱與沮喪，後來引申為身體不舒服。

A : You look exhausted. Are you feeling under the weather?

B : Not at all. I'm just preparing for my finals.

A : 你看起來很累，你感到身體不舒服嗎？

B : 一點也不，我只是正在為期末考做準備。

(三) 生病症狀

▶▶ # a bat in the cave 流鼻涕

洞穴裡的球棒，用 bat 來形容鼻涕，cave 來形容鼻孔。

A : As the weather is changing, I've got a bat in the cave.

A : Sounds like you need paper tissues to blow your nose.

A : 天氣變化不定，我流鼻涕了。

B : 聽起來你需要面紙來擦鼻涕。

▶▶ # be in pain 疼痛

A : My stomach is in pain and my legs have got a cramp.

B : Let me take a look at it.

A : 我的胃在痛，而我的腳在抽筋。

B : 讓我看一下吧。

▶▶ decayed tooth 蛀牙

decay 腐爛。

A：My teeth seem to be sensitive to heat and cold lately.

B：You should check to see if you have any decayed teeth.

A：我的牙齒最近似乎對熱和冷很敏感。

B：你應該檢查看是否有蛀牙。

▶▶ pass out 昏倒

A：Are you all right now? You scared me to death last night.

B：I passed out because I was exhausted. I badly need to catch up on some sleep.

A：你現在好些了嗎？昨晚你嚇死我了。

B：因為我太累，所以昏倒了。我很需要補充一些睡眠。

▶▶ ## run a fever 發燒

A : I am running a fever. I feel uncomfortable.

B : I'm sure you have a bad cold. Sometimes getting over your cold, it's best to stay in bed to rest.

A : 我在發燒，我感到不舒服。

B : 我肯定你得了重感冒。有時候要克服感冒，最好是在床上休息。

run a fever = have a fever

▶▶ ## running nose 流鼻涕

A : What happened to your nose?

B : I've got a running nose. It's killing me.

A : 你的鼻子怎麼了？

B : 我流鼻涕了，真難受。

▶▶ sore throat 喉嚨痛

sore 痛；throat 喉嚨。

A: The prescription is supposed to provide help for sore throats and reduce fever.

B: If the drug has any strong side effects, I wouldn't use it.

A: 這個處方應該是治療喉嚨痛和退燒。

B: 如果這種藥有任何強烈副作用，我不會服用它。

▶▶ throw up 嘔吐

A: My dog threw up and had diarrhea this morning.

B: You'd better take it to see the vet.

A: 今天早上我的狗嘔吐和腹瀉了。

B: 你最好帶牠去看獸醫。

throw up = vomit.

▶▶ stay off sb.'s foot 在床上休息

不下地走路，指在床上休息。

A: How long will it take to recover after surgery?

B: You may need to stay off your foot to help speed healing and spend less than three days in the hospital.

A: 手術後，要花多久的時間復原呢？

B: 你可能需要在床上休息來加速復原，且最少要住院3天。

(四) 生病治療

▶▶ do the trick 有效果

A: I don't know if the medicine can cure my allergies.

B: I think it should do the trick.

224

：我不知道這藥是否可以治療我的過敏症。

B ：我想它應該有效果。

補充

吃藥有效的句型有 It makes me feel better.（它讓我覺得好一點了。）

▶▶ go down 消腫

A ：My muscle swelled up after working out.

B ：You can put some ice on it until the swelling goes down.

A ：在運動後，我的肌肉都腫了。

B ：你可以上面敷一些冰直到消腫為止。

一般身體腫的句型 Your foot is swollen.（你的腳腫了。）

225

▶▶ get well 恢復

A : I heard you went to see the doctor for your illness. How did it go?

B : I will get well soon, as long as I take my medicine, drink more boiled water and have lots of rest, the doctor said.

A : 我聽說你生病去看醫生，那結果怎麼樣？

B : 醫生說，只要我吃藥、多喝開水和充足的休息，就會恢復得很快。

看醫生動詞一般用 see 或 consult。

▶▶ fill the prescription 抓藥

A : Could you take me to the drugstore to fill the prescription now?

B : You must be kidding. Don't you know it's snowing heavily outside?

A : 你現在能帶我去藥房抓藥嗎？

B : 你一定是開玩笑，你不知道外面在下大雪嗎？

▶▶ physical examination 身體檢查

A: How did the physical examination go?

B: Actually, not too good. The doctor wants me to check in the hospital and have some tests.

A: 你身體檢查結果如何？

B: 事實上，不太好，醫生要我住院做一些檢查。

補充

check in 住院；physical examination = checkup。

▶▶ over-the-counter 非處方藥

解說

在櫃檯銷售藥物，而不需處方，但可合法出售的現成藥。

A: I have a cold. I need to see the doctor.

B: If I were you, I might try some over-the-counter medications first.

A: 我感冒了，我需要看醫生。

B: 如果我是你，我會先試一些非處方藥。

227

PART

have a cold = catch (a) cold

▶▶ **take sb.'s temperature** 量某人的體溫

A : I feel I'm a little uncomfortable.

B : I think you should take your temperature, to make sure you are not running a fever.

A : 我覺得我有點不舒服。

B : 我想你應該量你的體溫,來確定你是不是在發燒。

▶▶ **recover from** 恢復

A : I need injection to help my fever go down.

B : I'm sorry to hear that. I hope you can recover from illness soon.

A : 我需要打針來幫助我退燒。

B : 聽到這個消息我感到難過,我希望你能很快恢復健康。

228

補充

give + ab. + a shot／an injection 給某人打針。

▶▶ **take medicine 吃藥**

解說

吃藥動詞要用 take。

A：How are you feeling?

B：I took some medicine, but it's making me very drowsy.

A：你現在感覺怎麼樣呢？

B：我吃了些藥，但是它讓我昏昏欲睡。

補充

一般吃藥常用句型 Take the medicine empty stomach.（空腹吃藥。）Take these medicine after meals.（飯後吃飯。）Take these medicine at bedtime.（睡前吃藥。）

▶▶ take these pills after sb.'s meal
飯後吃藥

pill 藥丸。

A : I feel nauseous after taking some pills. Maybe it's too strong for me.

B : You should read the label first. It says you take these pills after your meal.

A : 在吃些藥後，我想嘔吐，可能藥對我來說太猛了。

B : 你應該先讀標籤，它說飯後才吃藥。

▶▶ wait on 服侍（照顧）

A : You waited on me when I was sick. Thank you for everything you have done for me.

B : You're welcome. What are friends for?

A : 當我生病時，你照顧我，感謝你為我做的一切。

B : 不必客氣，不然朋友是當假的嗎？

PART

wait on = attend on

▶▶ **write out a prescription** 開藥方

 : The doctor wrote out a prescription for me. But it doesn't seem to help.

B : You can ask the doctor for a different prescription.

A : 醫生為我開了一個藥方，但是它似乎沒有效。

B : 你可以要求醫生開不同的處方。

補充

write out a prescription = give a prescription = prescribe a medicine = prescribe for an illness

04 情緒場景

(一) 心情好

 a million dollars 心情很好

A: I haven't seen you for a long time. How are you doing?

B: I feel like a million dollars.

A: 好久沒有看到你了，你還好嗎？

B: 我感覺心情很好。

補充

a million dollars 也有「十分健康」的意思，如 You look like a million dollars. 你看起來十分健康。

▶▶ **cheer up** （使某人）高興起來

A: This will be terrible because I didn't pass the pre-employment test.

B: Let's go out for dinner. That'll cheer you up.

A：這下糟糕了，因為我沒有通過職前考試。

B：我們出去吃飯吧，那樣會讓你高興些。

 in a good mood 心情好

A：I'm in a good mood now. Would you like to watch the fireworks with me tonight?

B：I'd love to, but I need to rehearsal for the presentation after work today.

A：找現在心情好，你今晚想要跟找去看煙火嗎？

B：我很想去，不過今天下班後，我需要演練簡報。

補充

心情不好可用 in a lousy / terrible / bad mood。

 on cloud nine 十分高興

解說

指高興像飛到九重雲霄。

: Why are you on cloud nine?

 : To be honest with you, I won a prize for my design.

 : 你為什麼這麼高興呢？

 : 老實跟你說，我設計得獎了。

▶▶ **on top of the world 十分高興**

解說

在世界的頂端，就會很得意，欣喜若狂。

 : Ever since I won that scholarship, I feel like I've been on top of the world.

 : I am happy you are doing so well.

 : 自從我得到獎學金後，我一直覺得十分高興。

 : 我很高興你表現得這麼好。

▶▶ seventh heaven 十分高興

(解)(說)

指高興像飛到七重天。

A: Since I met Jill, I've been in seventh heaven.

B: You two make a perfect match.

A: 自從我遇到吉兒,我一直心情十分高興。
B: 你們兩人是很好的一對。

 ▶▶ walk on air 十分高興

(解)(說)

形容人很高興,走路就像走在空氣中,有飄飄然的感覺。

A: She makes me feel like I'm walking on air.

B: I wish I had that connection with my girlfriend.

A: 她讓我覺得十分高興。
B: 我希望我跟我女朋友也有相同的感覺。

(二) 心情不好

▶▶ be upset 心煩

指難受或沮喪。

A : I'm upset about the test results.

B : Me, too. I thought I should have done better.

A : 我對考試的結果很心煩。
B : 我也是，我想我本應該考得更好才對。

▶▶ be down 情緒低落

A : I have been really down lately.

B : Why? Is everything ok at work?

A : 我最近情緒低落。
B : 為什麼呢？在工作上還好嗎？

be sick at heart 心裡非常難過

A : Since Betty left me, I've been really sick at heart.

B : Don't worry. There are many other fish in the sea.

A : 自從貝蒂離開我後，我一直心裡非常難過。

B : 不要擔心，天涯何處無芳草。

 down in the dumps 心情不好

解 說

dumps 情緒低落。

A : You have been absent-minded while in office.

B : I guess I feel down in the dumps about failing my project.

A : 在辦公室的時候，你有些心不在焉。

B : 我想是因為我的專案沒過，所以心情不好。

▶▶ heart-breaking 令人心碎的

A : It's a heart-breaking end to the movie that the two stars broke up.

B : It's only a movie, so don't get to upset.

A : 這部電影的結局令人心碎，兩個主角分手了。

B : 它只是一部電影，所以不要傷心。

▶▶ look blue 神色沮喪

blue 憂鬱的。

A : You look blue. What's going on?

B : I don't feel so good.

A：你看起來神色沮喪，發生了什麼事？

B：我覺得不舒服。

▶▶ feel blue 感到無精打采

A：Ever since my dog died, I have been feeling blue.

B：I am sorry to hear about Toby.

A：自從我的狗死後，我一直感到無精打采。

B：我很抱歉聽到關於托比的死訊。

▶▶ in a low spirit 心情低落

A：If I fail one more time, I am laid off by my employer.

B：No wonder you are in a low spirit.

A：如果我再失敗一次，我會被我的雇主開除。

B：難怪你心情低落。

▶▶ long face 愁眉苦臉

A : Why the long face?

B : I was just fired from my job.

> **A** : 為什麼愁眉苦臉呢？
> **B** : 我剛被解僱了。

▶▶ out of spirits 沒精神

A : You look like you're out of spirits. What's up with you?

B : My boss didn't like the organization I chose.

> **A** : 你看起來沒什麼精神，你發生了什麼事？
> **B** : 我的老闆不喜歡我選的機構。

類似句型 My boss didn't like the candidates we interviewed.（我的老闆不喜歡我們面試的求職者。）

▶▶ **out of sorts** 心情不好

來自以前印刷時，排字工人發覺鉛字（sort）不齊全，就會不高興。

A : Ever since Mary lost the promotion, she has been out of sorts.

B : I'm sure she will be ok after a little time goes by.

A : 自從瑪麗沒有獲得升遷，她就一直心情不好。

B : 我相信她過不久就會沒事。

(三) 生氣

▶▶ **be hot under the collar** 發怒

指領子下面是熱呼呼的，只有很生氣時，才會這樣。

A : I'm hot under the collar because someone stole my camera.

B : Who do you think it may have been?

A²：我很生氣，因為有人偷走我的相機。

B²：你認為可能是誰偷的呢？

補充

相同片語有 get hot under the collar。

▶▶ fit to be tied 非常生氣

：I'm fit to be tied because I still haven't gotten my stuff back from Susan.

B²：You should offer her an ultimatum.

A²：我非常生氣，因為我還沒有從蘇珊那裡拿回我的東西。

B²：你應該給她下最後通牒。

▶▶ get in sb.'s hair 激怒某人

解說

爬到某人頭上，表示干擾到別人，促使某人生氣。

242

: Do they bother your study?

B : They surely do. They really get in my hair.

 : 他們有打擾到你的工作嗎？

B : 當然有啊，他們真的激怒我了。

▶▶ hit the ceiling 生氣

(解)(說)

指勃然大怒。

 : Angel still hasn't gotten her salary back.

B : Yes. She really hit the ceiling with her boss.

 : 安琪兒還沒有拿到她的薪水。

B : 沒錯，她很生她老闆的氣。

(補)(充)

hit the ceiling 中的 hit 可用 raise 替換，ceiling 可用 roof 替換，
其意思都不變。

▶▶ lose sb.'s temper 生氣

A: The camera I borrowed from Tina was stolen.

B: She's really going to lose her temper when she finds out.

A: 我向蒂娜借來的相機被偷了。

B: 當她知道時，她真的會很生氣。

 補充

lose sb.'s temper = lose sb.'s cool

▶▶ make sb.'s blood boil 使某人憤怒

A: Mary really makes my blood boil.

B: Why does she make you so upset?

A: 瑪麗真的讓我憤怒。

B: 她為什麼讓你心煩呢？

PART

▶▶ raise the roof 生氣

A: I accidentally damaged Tom's car.

B: With his temper, he really raises the roof.

> **A:** 我不小心弄壞湯姆的車子了。
> **B:** 按照他的脾氣，他真的會很生氣。

▶▶ rub sb. the wrong way 激怒某人

A: What you told Mary really rubbed her the wrong way.

B: She must have misunderstood me, because I didn't mean for her to get upset.

> **A:** 你對瑪麗講的話真的激怒她了。
> **B:** 她一定誤解我了，因為我不是故意要惹她生氣的。

補充

rub sb. the right way 使某人高興。

245

▶▶ **step on sb.'s toes** 觸怒某人

踩了某人的腳，表示觸怒某人或得罪某人。

A : If you knew what was good for you, you wouldn't step on her toes.

B : Maybe you're right. I should calm down and handle this matter civilly.

A : 如果你早知道什麼對你有利，你就不會觸怒她了。

B : 或許你說得對，我應該冷靜下來，理性地處理這件事。

▶▶ **take sth. out on sb.** 對某人發脾氣

A : What a day! I'm really worn out. Just buzz off and leave me alone.

B : Well, there's no need to take it out on me.

A': 多麼糟的一天！我真的很累，走開，讓我清靜一下。

B': 嗯，不需要對我發脾氣。

buzz off 滾開。

▶▶ **vent sth. to sb.** 對某人吐露或發洩某事

用在指感情或情緒上的吐露或發洩。

A': Earlier today, Mary came and vented her problems to me.

B': Is she going to be ok?

A': 今天早一點的時候，瑪麗來對我吐露她的困難。

B': 她還好吧？

(四) 緊張

▶▶ be afraid of sb.'s own shadow
提心吊膽

A: Stop being afraid of your own shadow, and tell her how you feel.

B: I would, but she is an intimidating person.

A: 你不要提心吊膽,告訴她你的感覺。

B: 我會的,可是她是一個令人生畏的人。

▶▶ butterflies in sb.'s stomach 緊張

直譯為「蝴蝶在肚子裡」,會很噁心,形容人在上臺或表演前,會緊張,造成胃部不舒服。

A: As it's almost time to present our special guests, I'm getting butterflies in my stomach.

B: Just be yourself. I believe your presentation will be fascinating.

A : 呈現給我們重要客人的時間快到了，我很緊張。

B : 只要做回你自己，我相信你的簡報會很精彩。

▶▶ **get cold feet** 緊張

解說
指人一緊張就兩腳冰冷。

A : I'll be nervous when I'm beset by reporters at the meeting.

B : There's no need to get cold feet. The meeting will be finished soon.

A : 當我在會議中被記者包圍時，我很緊張。

B : 不用緊張，這會議會很快就結束。

▶▶ **like a cat on hot bricks** 急促不安

解說
直譯為「像熱磚上的貓」，急促不安，相當於熱鍋裡的螞蟻。

A: Why are you like a cat on hot bricks?

B: I lost my wallet with my credit cards, ID and 1,000 bucks in it.

A: 為什麼你急促不安呢？

B: 我遺失我的錢包，裡面有我的信用卡、身分證和 1,000美元。

▶▶ on edge 緊張

A: You seem on edge. What happened to you?

B: Today they'll announce the winning entry in this year's logo contest.

A: 你似乎很緊張，你發生了什麼事？

B: 今天他們會宣布今年商標比賽獲獎名單。

▶▶ on pins and needles 急切期盼

直譯為「在大頭針與針的上面」，好像如坐針氈，急切期盼。

A : Why didn't you keep your mind on the office this morning?

B : I waited on pins and needles for the results of Monday's contest.

A : 你早上為什麼不能專心上班呢？

B : 我急切期盼等待星期一競賽結果。

補充

其他緊張片語：shake all over ／ get sb.'s tongue tied ／ have sb.'s mind go blank。

(五) 放鬆

▶▶ **cool it** 放鬆下來

A : I am so stressed out about the results of yesterday's interview.

B : You need to just cool it. The interview is over now, and you will find out the result soon enough.

A : 我對於昨天的面試結果壓力很大。

B : 你只需要放鬆一點，現在面試結束了，你很快就會知道結果。

▶▶ take it easy 放輕鬆

A : I was very nervous during the interview. I didn't know what to say.

B : Take it easy. It is all over now.

> **A** : 在面試的時候，我很緊張，我不知道該說些什麼。
>
> **B** : 放輕鬆，一切都結束了。

▶▶ breathe easily 鬆一口氣

A : I was so nervous about the interview.

B : Now that it's over, you can breathe easily.

> **A** : 我對於面試很緊張。
>
> **B** : 既然面試結束了，你可以鬆一口氣。

▶▶ hold sb.'s horse 別急

A：The road is jammed with cars. I'm afraid that we are going to miss the flight.

B：Hold your horses. We can take a detour.

A：道路塞車，我擔心我們會沒趕上班機。

B：別急，我們可以繞路走。

補充

1. 塞車常用片語有 rush hour（上下班的尖峰時刻）／ heavy traffic（交通流量大）、light traffic（交通流量小）／ traffic lights（紅綠燈）
2. 塞車常用句型 The traffic is tied up.（交通堵塞了。）／ The traffic is backed up.（交通堵塞了。）

▶▶ play it cool 保持冷靜

A：I don't know what I should say to them.

B：Just play it cool, and tell them what they want to hear.

A：我不知道該對他們說些什麼。

B：保持冷靜，告訴他們想要聽的事。

PART

05 時間場景

(一) 慢

▶▶ for a little 一會兒

解說
指經過很短的時間。

A：Could you stay for a little while?

B：I'd love to, but I'm afraid I would miss the bus.

A：你能停留一會兒嗎？
B：我很願意，但是我害怕我會趕不上公車。

▶▶ for a moment 一會兒

A：Will you please look after my luggage for a moment?

B：Sure.

 ： 請你看管我的行李一會兒好嗎？

 ： 當然可以。

▶▶ just a minute 等一會

解說

指稍等片刻。

A ： It's getting late. I'm afraid I've got to leave.

B ： Just a minute. Let me give you a ride.

A ： 已經很晚了，恐怕我該走了。

B ： 等一會，我開車送你吧。

補充

just a minute = just a second = wait a minute = just hang on a minute
= hold on a minute

PART

(二) 快

▶▶ **at once** 立刻

 I don't feel so well.

 You should go home at once.

 我感覺到不舒服。
 你應該立刻回家。

▶▶ **in a flash** 立刻

解說
flash 閃光。

 I'll be there at once. I'm running late.

 I'll be done with my make-up in a flash.

 我要立刻去那裡，我快遲到了。
 我會立刻打扮完畢。

▶▶ **in a minute** 立刻 / 馬上

minute 分，表示很短的時間。

A：It's time for dinner, Curtis.

B：Ok. I'll be there in a minute.

A：柯帝斯，晚餐時間到了。

B：好的，我馬上就過去。

▶▶ **in next to no time at all** 立刻

此片語可縮寫爲 in no time。

A：She seems to have made new friends in next to no time at all.

B：Sure. She's an easy-going person.

A：她似乎很快交到了新朋友。

B：沒錯，她是很隨和的人。

▶▶ make it 及時到達

A：I doubt if I can make it to the office on time.

B：Well, you need to get here as soon as possible.

A：我懷疑是否能準時到達辦公室。

B：嗯，你需要盡快趕到這裡。

補充

1. make it 有成功或做完某事的意思，如 I believe you can make it as long as you work hard and do your level best. 只要你努力工作和盡全力，我相信你可以成功。
2. on time 是「準時」的意思，指剛好在預定的時間；in time 是「及時」的意思，指在預定時間內前幾分鐘到達。

▶▶ on time 準時

A：The director said next Monday is the deadline for handing in the design proposals.

B：I hope I can finish it on time.

A：主管說，下星期一是繳交設計提案的最後期限。

B：我希望可以準時完成設計提案。

▶▶ on short notice 急忙

指強調在很短的時間內。

A : I will be right over to help you with your problems.

B : Thanks for coming on such short notice.

A : 我馬上就來幫忙你處理問題。

B : 謝謝你如此急忙地趕過來。

補 充

on short notice = at short notice

▶▶ on the spur of the moment 立刻

指一時衝動，不假思索。

A : I decided to go to Hawaii on the spur of the moment.

B : Have you thought about what you will do when you arrive there?

A: 我決定立刻去夏威夷。

B: 你有想過,當你到達那裡,你打算做什麼呢?

(三) 開始

▶▶ **get cracking** 開始

解說

指迅速著手開始工作。

A: What do you kill time after resignation?

B: I plan to get cracking on this new job, so I can make some money, and gain some experience.

A: 離職後,你會做什麼來消磨時間呢?

B: 我計畫開始做這項新工作,那麼我就可以賺一些錢並得到一些經驗。

▶▶ **get off the ground** 順利開始

解說

指活動或事業一開始就很順利。

A : Without your help, the project would never get off the ground.

B : You're welcome. It's my pleasure.

A : 沒有你的幫忙，專案就無法開始起步。

B : 別客氣，這是我的榮幸。

▶▶ in the first place 首先

A : Do you know anything about e-commerce?

B : In the first place, I have taken classes on e-commerce.

A : 你懂電子商務嗎？

B : 首先，我有上過電子商務的課程。

▶▶ kick off 開始

A : It's about time to kick off the project.

B : I have no objection, but who can finish it in one day?

 PART

A：到了該開始執行計畫的時候了。

B：我沒有意見，不過誰能在一天內完成它？

▶▶ turn over a new leaf 改過自新

A：I heard Mike has turned over a new leaf and he will not skip the class anymore.

B：Good news. I hope he can stick to it.

A：我聽說麥克已經改過自新，他不會再蹺課。

B：好消息，我希望他能堅持住。

(四) 結束

▶▶ after all 畢竟

強調最終的意思。

A：The company hasn't gone out of business after all.

B：It's only a matter of time. So now I need to keep something for a rainy day, just in case.

A：畢竟這家公司還沒有破產。

B：只是時間上的問題，所以現在我需要未雨綢繆，以防萬一。

▶▶ call it a day 收工

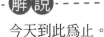

今天到此為止。

A：I'm pooped because I'm overworked.

B：Me, too. It's time to call it a day.

A：因為工作過度，我是精疲力竭。

B：我也是，該是收工的時間到了。

▶▶ end up 結果

常指不好的結果。

A: I want to excel in this field but end up getting nowhere.

B: After taking a good holiday, try it again and maybe you will get more accomplished.

A: 我想要在這領域中得到進展,但是結果卻無進展。

B: 度過愉快地假期後,然後再試一下,說不定你會有更多的收穫。

▶▶ in the end 最後

A: I heard our colleagues are interested in attending the finance conference.

B: That may be what they said, but I think they won't like to pay the expensive registration fees in the end.

A: 我聽說我們的同事有興趣參加財務研討會。

B: 他們可能是說說而已,但我想他們最後不會願意付昂貴的報名費。

▶▶ over and done with 結束

解說

強調已經結束。

A : My presentation is over and done with. What did you think?

B : It was pretty good, but it could have been better.

A : 我的簡報已經結束了，你覺得怎麼樣呢？

B : 它很好，但是它應該能更好。

▶▶ put a stop to 使…停止

A : Let's eat out at McDonald's tonight.

B : You'd better put a stop to that idea immediately because McDonald's isn't good for you.

A : 我們今晚在麥當勞吃飯吧。

B : 你最好立刻停止那種想法，因為吃麥當勞對你健康不好。

▶▶ put an end to 結束

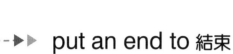: I can't believe you are here instead of being in Vancouver.

B : The blizzard put an end to the trip.

A : 我無法相信你在這裡而不是在溫哥華。

B : 這場暴風雪結束了這次旅行。

06 購物消費

(一) 便宜

▶▶ dirt cheap 非常便宜

A: Is the Swatch watch outrageously expensive?

B: Not at all. It's dirt cheap.

A: 這只 Swatch 手錶很昂貴嗎？

B: 一點也不，它非常便宜。

▶▶ get bargains 低價購買

解說

意思是說以較低的價錢買到商品；bargain 便宜貨。

A: How can you get bargains on luxury products?

B: I always buy ones during the year-end clearance sale.

A： 你如何低價購買奢侈品呢？

B： 我經常在年終清倉拍賣中購買奢侈品。

(二) 很貴

▶▶ **be steep** 價格太貴

A： Consumer prices are soaring again.

B： No wonder I even feel the price of toothpaste is steep.

A： 消費者物價再度上漲。

B： 難怪，我甚至覺得牙膏價格很貴。

a steal 價格很便宜。

▶▶ **highway robbery** 敲竹槓

A： I bought the coffee set for ten bucks.

B： Too expensive. That's highway robbery.

A : 我花了10元買這組咖啡用具。

B : 太貴了，那是敲竹槓啊。

▶▶ # rip-off 敲詐

A : I have to buy the text for the American Literature class. It will cost me 50 bucks.

B : That's a rip-off. It is not worth so much.

A : 我必須買美國文學課的教科書，它要花我50元。

B : 真是敲詐啊，它不值那麼多錢。

(三) 免費

▶▶ # free of charge 免費

A : How much does this newspaper cost?

B : The cost is $1.00. But you may elect to read it online free of charge.

A : 這份報紙多少錢？

B : 價錢是一美元，但是你可以選擇在線上免費閱讀。

▶▶ for nothing 免費

A : It was very kind of you to offer me your books for nothing.

B : Don't mention it.

A : 你人真好，免費送我你的書。

B : 別客氣。

▶▶ give away 贈送

A : I have to move into a new apartment but don't have space for all of my things.

B : Are you giving anything away?

A : 我必須搬到一個新的公寓，可是沒有空間容納我所有的東西。

B : 你正在送東西嗎？

▶▶ next to nothing 幾乎免費

A : The store offered a coupon for $20.00 off, so I got the walkman for next to nothing.

B : Sounds like you got a good deal.

> **A** : 這家商店提供免費20美元折價券，所以我買這臺隨身聽幾乎免費。
>
> **B** : 聽起來好像你買得真便宜。

(四) 其他

▶▶ a waste of money 浪費金錢

A : I want to buy those new Nike shoes.

B : It would be a waste of money to spend that much money on sneakers.

> **A** : 我想要買那雙新的耐吉鞋子。
>
> **B** : 花那麼多錢買運動鞋真是浪費金錢。

▶▶ be short of 缺少

A: I want to buy a brand new computer, but I'm a little short of cash.

B: Now is hardly the time for you to buy an expensive computer.

A: 我想要買一臺全新的電腦,可是我缺一些現金。

B: 現在根本不是你買一臺昂貴電腦的時機。

be short of = be lack of

▶▶ check out 看一下

此片語常用在看美好的事物或看美女與帥哥。

A: Check out the new shoes I just bought.

B: Nice! How much did you spend on them?

A: 看一下我剛買的新鞋子。

B: 很漂亮,你買新鞋子花了多少錢呢?

▶▶ for sale 待售

指廉價出售。

A: I heard the car is for sale.

B: Sure. The price is 10% cheaper than it was yesterday. So, you'd better hurry if you still want it.

A: 我聽說這輛車子正在待售。

B: 沒錯,這個價格比昨天便宜10%;所以如果你還想要它,你最好快一點。

▶▶ garage sale 車庫拍賣

A: Why do you always shop at a garage sale?

B: My finances are really low. I need to buy stuff at a low price.

A: 你為什麼總是在車庫拍賣中購物呢?

B: 我的財務狀況真的不好,我需要以低的價格來買東西。

▶▶ invest in 買

強調買東西是有投資的意味。

A: The TV picture is fuzzy tonight. Something is wrong with it.

B: It's about time to invest in a new one.

A: 今晚電視畫面很不清晰,這臺電視有點問題。

B: 該買一臺新電視的時候到了。

▶▶ on the rise 上漲

A: The price of gas is on the rise.

B: I know. I think I will buy a hybrid car to save on gas.

A: 汽油價格正在上漲。

B: 我知道,我想我會買一輛油電混合車來省油。

▶▶ trade sth. in for 汰舊換新

trade in 抵價購物。

A: My iPad is always breaking down. I've had enough of it.

B: You can trade it in for a new one during the sale season.

A: 我的平板電腦老是故障,我已經受夠了。

B: 你可以在打折季裡以汰舊換新方式買一部。

▶▶ window shopping 逛街

只逛不買東西。

A: Let's go window shopping.

B: I know there is a nice place to browse on Broadway.

A：我們去逛街吧。

B：我知道百老匯有一個閒逛的好地方。

▶▶ **wrap up** 包紮 / 打包

指包起來。

A：I need to wrap the books up in brown paper and string. Do you have them?

B：No, I don't have them. But you can try Mike.

A：我需要用牛皮紙和繩子來打包書，你有那些東西嗎？

B：不，我沒有那些東西，但是你可以問一下麥克。

第
3
單元

職場旅遊場景片語

01 機場

02 餐廳

03 出差飯店住宿

04 放輕鬆

05 興趣

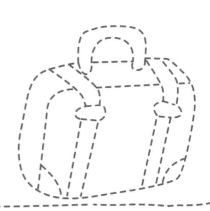

PART

01 機場

▶▶ **airsick bag** 嘔吐袋

A : I feel airsick. Please give me an airsick bag.

B : Here it is.

A : 我暈機，請給我嘔吐袋。
B : 給你。

▶▶ **Attention, please?** 請注意

這裡的 attention 是 May I have your attention? 的縮寫。

A : Attention, please? Flight 19 is leaving at 11:30 a.m.

B : All right. We will now begin boarding.

A : 請注意，航班19將在早上11點30分離開。
B : 好的，我們現在要開始登機了。

▶▶ bail out 放棄

A : I am sorry I had to bail out on you last night, because I had to pick up my girlfriend from the airport.

B : Don't sweat it. We can hang out next weekend.

A : 對不起,我放棄昨晚和你的聚會,因為我必須去機場接我的女朋友。

B : 別緊張,我們下週末可以聚一聚。

hang out 在一起;bail out = give up。

▶▶ be included in 包括在

A : What's included in your ticket?

B : The food and beverages are free on the flight because they'll be included in your ticket.

A : 什麼費用包括在機票裡?

B : 班機上的食物與飲料都是免費的,因為費用都包括在機票裡。

▶▶ be open to 對…開放

A: The lounge is open to all passengers. Come here if you want to rest.

B: That will be great if the lounge offer free Wi-Fi.

A: 這休息室是對所有乘客開放，只要你想要休息，就來這裡。

B: 如果休息室有提供免費無線上網，那就會很棒。

▶▶ book a ticket 預訂機票

餐廳訂位也用 book 動詞，如訂位 book a table。

A: I've booked a ticket from Taipei to Singapore. I want to confirm my seat now.

B: Sure. May I have your name and flight number, please?

PART

A : 我已經預訂一張從臺北到新加坡的機票,現在我要確認我的機位。

B : 沒問題,請告訴我你的名字和航班號碼?

 ▶▶ **clear up** 解決問題

(解)(說)
指消除誤會或解決問題。

A : I had a flight reservation for tomorrow night, and my ticket states it's for tonight.

B : I am terribly sorry, sir. I'll clear this up for you right away.

A : 我訂明晚的機位,但是我的票上顯示是今晚。

B : 先生,很對不起,我會立刻為你解決這個問題。

▶▶ **confirm a flight** 確認航班

A : I'd like to confirm a flight, please.

B : Certainly, sir. May I have your name, flight number and date of departure, please?

A: 我想要確認航班，拜託一下。

B: 先生，當然可以，請告訴我你的名字、班機號碼和起飛日期？

▶▶ **economy class** 經濟艙

飛機的座位分為經濟艙、商務艙與頭等艙三種，其價位為經濟艙＜商務艙＜頭等艙。

A: Would you like to fly economy class or first class?

B: I'd like to travel first class, please.

A: 你想要搭乘經濟艙或頭等艙呢？

B: 我想要搭乘頭等艙，謝謝。

▶▶ either...or 不是…就是

A: Your baggage is overweight by 2 kilos. You have two options either pay for excess baggage or remove it from your baggage.

B: I think I choose to pay the excess baggage charges.

A: 你的行李超重2公斤，你有兩種選擇，不是付超重費就是移除超重行李。

B: 我想我還是選擇付超重行李費。

▶▶ aisle seat 靠道座位

A: Would you like an aisle seat or a window seat?

B: I prefer window seat, please.

A: 你想要坐靠道座位或靠窗座位呢？

B: 我較喜歡靠窗座位，謝謝。

leave sth. under sb.'s seat
放某物在座椅底下

A：Oh, no. My carry-on luggage is too big for the locker.

B：Why not leave it under your seat?

> A：糟了，我的手提行李太大，行李櫃裡放不下。
>
> B：為何不放在座椅底下呢？

make a reservation 訂票

指預訂。

A：How may I help you?

B：I'd like to make a reservation to New York.

> A：有什麼能為你效勞嗎？
>
> B：我想要訂一張到紐約的機票。

make a reservation = book a ticket

▶▶ **on schedule** 準時

按時間表，強調準時。

A : When is the departure time?

B : On schedule, in 30 minutes.

A : 起飛時間是何時？

B : 準時，在30分鐘後。

on schedule = on time

▶▶ **one-way trip** 單程

A : What's the fare for a one-way trip to London?

B : Sorry, I don't know the right price now, but please refer to the price list on our website.

PART

A：到倫敦的單程票價是多少？

B：抱歉，目前我不知道正確價格，但是你可以參考我們網站的價格表。

補充

1. fare 是「票價」的意思，用在 bus fare（公車票）、train fare（火車票）、airfare／air ticket（飛機票）。
2. round trip 來回；refer to 參考。

 ▶▶ **queue up to board 排隊登機**

解說

在英國排隊都用 queue，在美國用 line，所以 queue up to board = line up to board。

A：Please queue up to board. The boarding gate will be closed 10 minutes before departure time.

B：Come on, we have got to walk fast or we're going to miss our flight.

A：請排隊登機，這登機門會在起飛前10分鐘關閉。

B：快一點，我們必須走快一點，否則我們會錯過我們的航班。

▶▶ stop over 中途停留

 解 說

指飛行旅程中的中途停留。

A : You are stopping over in Singapore for one night on your way to Sydney.

B : I see.

A : 在去雪梨的旅程中，你會在新加坡中途停留一晚。

B : 我知道。

▶▶ vegetarian meal 素食餐

A : We are serving dinner now. What can I get you?

B : I choose the vegetarian meal. It is the best meal my friend has ever had.

A : 我們現在供應晚餐，你要點什麼呢？

B : 我選擇素食餐，它是我朋友曾經吃過最好吃的餐點。

PART

▶▶ waiting list 候補名單

A: I want to make a reservation on tomorrow night's flight.

B: Sorry, Mr. Wang. The flight is completely booked. I can put you on a waiting list if you would like.

A: 我想要訂明天晚上的班機。

B: 抱歉，王先生，這班機已訂滿了，如果你願意，我可以把你排在等候名單。

▶▶ watch sb.'s step 小心一點

直譯為注意某人的腳，引申為小心一點。

A: My seat is 10A.Could you direct me to my seat?

B: Sure. Go straight and please watch your step. Another hostess will show you to your seat.

A': 我的座位是10A，你能指引我的座位嗎？

B': 當然可以，直走和小心點走，另一位空服員會帶
領你到你的座位。

direct to 是強調直接指示，show + sb. to + somewhere 將某人帶
到某地。

 02 餐廳

▶▶ **be my guest** 請便

A : May I eat the dessert?

B : Be my guest.

A : 我能吃點心嗎？

B : 別客氣，請便。

 補充

喝湯動詞要用 eat，比如 Eat more soup.（湯多喝點。），喝飲料動詞要用 drink，比如 Drink a beer.（喝一杯啤酒。）

▶▶ **be on sb.** 某人請客

A : Dinner is on me.

B : Fantastic.

A : 晚餐我請客。

B : 太棒了。

補 充

類似說法有 I buy you dinner.（晚餐我請客。）、I treat you.（我招待你。）

▶▶ **be plenty of** 很多

A : Have some more cake. There are plenty of cakes left.

B : Thanks. I'm full.

A : 再多吃些蛋糕啊。有剩很多蛋糕。

B : 謝謝，我飽ㄌ。

補 充

go to waste 被浪費掉，比如 Not to let a free meal go to waste.（不要讓免費的食物被浪費。）

▶▶ **book a table** 訂位

A : I'd like to book a table for ten at seven tonight.

B : Sorry, We're booked out.

A : 我想要訂今晚一張10人一桌的座位。

B : 抱歉，我們客滿了。

PART

補充

We're booked out. = We're full booked.

▶▶ **consist of** 由…做的 / 由…構成 / 含有

Ａ: What does the salad consist of?

Ｂ: It consist of tomatoes, red onions and cucumbers.

Ａ: 沙拉含有什麼呢？

Ｂ: 沙拉含有番茄、紅色洋蔥和黃瓜。

▶▶ **count sb. in** 算某人一份

解說

指把某人計算在內；而相反詞為 count sb. out（不要算我在內）。

Ａ: We're going out for pizza tonight. Do you want to come?

Ｂ: I'm starving. Count me in.

Ａ: 我們今晚要外出吃比薩，你想要一起去嗎？

Ｂ: 我很餓，算我一份。

292

▶▶ eat out 出外吃飯

eat out = dine out；eat in（在家吃飯）= dine in

A : We are looking for a place where we can eat out.

B : I know a good place on the wrong side of shopping mall.

A : 我們正在尋找我們可以出外吃飯的餐廳。

B : 我知道有一間好餐廳在購物中心的左邊。

▶▶ fill with 塞滿

A : What is the roasted duck filled with?

B : It's filled with the seasoning and spices.

A : 烤鴨中塞滿了什麼？

B : 牠塞滿了調味調與香料。

調味料是有季節性，會隨四季不同而變化，於是調味料為 season（季節）+ ing = seasoning，而 seasoning 和 dressing 都是調味料，seasoning 是指風乾後的調味料，如 seasoning powder（調味粉），而 dressing 是指溼的調味料，如 salad dressing（生菜食品的調味汁）。

▶▶ full up 吃飽

A : Are you full up?

B : I'm stuffed.

A : 你吃飽了嗎？

B : 我吃飽了。

▶▶ get in 進入

A : How about the French place?

B : We can't get in without a reservation.

A : 去吃這家法國餐廳如何呢？

B : 沒有預約我們進不去。

餐廳情境常用片語 affordable price 優惠價格、be made with 用什麼製作、hand-made 手做的、main dish 主菜、self-service restaurant 自助餐廳、staff cafeteria 員工餐廳。

▶▶ go out for dinner 外出吃飯

A : Let's go out for dinner tonight.

B : My thoughts exactly.

A : 讓我們今晚外出吃飯吧。

B : 我正有此意。

1. 餐廳常用句型 What is the house specialty?（餐廳特色菜是什麼？）Would you bring me the menu, please?（請你給我菜單好嗎？）What is your favorite main course?（什麼是你最喜歡的主菜？）
2. 食物的味道有 acid（酸）、sweet（甜）、bitter（苦）、spicy（辣的）、bland（味道淡）、tangy（味道濃）。
3. 味道有 flavor 與 aroma 兩種，flavor 指嚐起來的味道，而 aroma 指聞起來的味道。

▶▶ hit the spot 好吃

A : How is the dessert?

B : It hits the spot.

A : 點心味道如何呢?

B : 它很好吃。

一般形容東西好吃的說法有:
1. It's delicious / incredible / juicy / tasty.
2. It really tastes good.
3. It's out of the world.
4. It couldn't be better.

▶▶ in a minute 立刻

A : Can you please order for me?

B : I'll be with you in a minute.

A : 你能為我點菜嗎?

B : 我立刻就過來。

▶▶ lose track of 沒有注意到

A : Why didn't you show up in the snack bar two hours ago?

B : Something came up, and I lost track of the time.

A : 你為什麼兩小時前沒有到小吃店呢？

B : 剛好有事，而我沒有注意到時間。

▶▶ no good 沒有用

強調沒有價值，此片語後面要接動名詞。

A : It's no good looking at me like that. I am not going to forgive you that easily.

B : What if I take you to the most romantic restaurant in town?

A : 那樣看我是沒有用，我不會那麼輕易原諒你。

B : 如果我帶你去城裡最浪漫的餐廳如何？

PART

▶▶ stay on 繼續停留

用在別人離開後或超出自己的預定時間後而留下來。

A : We are planning to go to the snack bar after work. Do you want to come?

B : I'd love to, but I must stay on here and finish the job.

A : 下班後，我們打算要去小吃店？你想要一起來嗎？

B : 我很想，但是我必須繼續停留在這裡完成這工作。

▶▶ take sb. to 帶某人去

A : I don't know where to take my client to lunch.

B : How about a Japanese place?

A : 我不知道帶我的客戶去哪邊吃中餐。

B : 去日本餐廳吃如何呢？

補充

How about...? （你認為如何），用在提出建議時使用。

 take out or for here 外帶或內用

解說

類似的說法有 take out or take in 或 to go or for here。

A : Hi, take out or for here?

B : Take out, please.

A : 嗨，外帶或內用呢？

B : 外帶，謝謝。

 work on 練習

A : Nancy is taking me to the best restaurant in town tonight.

B : You'd better work on your dining etiquette, before you go.

A: 南茜今晚會帶我去城裡最好的餐廳。

B: 在你去之前，你最好練習一下你的餐桌禮儀。

▶▶ **a piece of work** 陰險

可以指一件作品，但在口語中 a (nasty) piece of work 形容人很
陰險。

A²: He almost had me fooled. I really believed that
I was going to receive a free vacation.

B²: Those scam artists are a real piece of work.
Remember, if it sounds too good to be true, it
probably is.

A²: 他幾乎把我給騙了，我真的相信我會得到一個免
費的假期。

B²: 那些詐騙高手真是陰險呀，記住，如果事情聽起
來好得令人難以置信，那麼它很有可能不是真
的。

scam 詐騙，artist 高手，too good to be true 太好未必是眞的。

▶▶ above all 最重要的是

A : Why do you go to Beijing?

B : I want to see the Forbidden City, but above all, I'm going on business.

> A : 你為什麼去北京呢？
>
> B : 我想要去看紫禁城，但是最重要的是，我是去出差。

▶▶ book in / into 入住

指入住旅館登記，而 book 是向旅館、飯店、戲院等做預約。

A : I want to book myself into your hotel tonight.

B : Sorry, we're fully booked.

> A : 我今晚想入住你們的旅館。
>
> B : 抱歉，我們全客滿了。

1. 旅館情境常見片語 be located close to（位於什麼附近）、check in 報到、check out 離開、complimentary breakfast 附贈早餐、room service 客房服務、room rate 房價、settle the check 付帳單、wake-up call 起床叫醒電話。
2. 旅館情境常見句型 Do you have a reservation?（你有預訂嗎？）Does the room rate inlude breakfast?（房價有包括早餐嗎？）Does the hotel have a minibus service?（旅館有小巴服務嗎？）How can I make a booking on line?（我如何線上預訂房間呢？）Is there wireless Internet in the hotel?（旅館有無線網路嗎？）Is parking available?（有停車位嗎？）

▶▶ **call dibs on 有權**

用在你有權要求怎麼樣或怎麼做。

A : Cool! The hotel room has bunk beds.

B : I call dibs on the top bunk.

A : 真棒！這旅館房間有上下鋪。

B : 我有權睡上鋪。

▶▶ go abroad 出國

A: I heard you are going to go abroad. Is that true?

B: Yes, it's true. I'm leaving for Rome in a fortnight.

A: 我聽說你要出國,是真的嗎?

B: 沒錯,是真的,兩週後我要去羅馬。

▶▶ keep the change 不用找零錢

A: Here is ten bucks. You can keep the change.

B: Thanks a lot. Do you want a hand with that heavy suitcase?

A: 這裡是10元,你不用找零錢。

B: 謝謝,你需要我幫你提沉重的手提箱嗎?

▶▶ line up 排隊

A: I was able to line up early to buy tickets for the Phantom of the Opera on Friday.

B: Awesome. I cannot wait to see the play.

> **A:** 我星期五能夠早點去排隊買歌劇魅影的票。
>
> **B:** 太好了，我等不及看這表演。

▶▶ leave sth. in the hands 交給

A: I am looking for someone to watch my dog while I'm on vacation.

B: Don't leave the responsibility in my hands. I'm allergic to dogs.

> **A:** 我要去度假，我正在找人來照顧我的狗。
>
> **B:** 不要交給我，我對狗過敏。

補充

on vacation 度假、be allergic to 對…過敏。

PART

▶▶ put up 投宿

為某人提供膳宿。

A: Where are they putting you up when you are on business in New York?

B: A hotel called the Palace.

> **A:** 當你在紐約出差時,他們安排你投宿哪裡呢?
> **B:** 一間叫宮殿的旅館。

▶▶ single or double

你想要訂單人房或雙人房呢?

single or double 為 Would you like to book a single or double room?
整句的簡化;double room 雙人房(只有一張雙人的床)、twin room 雙人房(是指有兩張小床)。

A: Single or double?

B: Which is cheaper?

A: 你想要訂單人房或雙人房呢？

B: 哪一個房間較便宜呢？

▶▶ suitable for 適合

A: Can you recommend a hotel in Oxford suitable for business trip?

B: Sure. What's your budget like?

A: 你能推薦在牛津適合商業旅行的旅館嗎？

B: 當然可以，你的預算是多少？

補充

一般旅館對話常會用的表達有：lobby 旅館大廳、front desk 前臺、morning call 叫醒服務、room service 客房服務。

▶▶ stay at 投宿

解說

強調短暫的居住；類似常用的句子有 Which hotel will you be staying in?（你將住什麼旅館呢？）

Ａ：Which hotel do you stay at when you're in To-kyo?

Ｂ：I stay at the super hotel.

Ａ：當你在東京時，你會投宿哪一間旅館？
Ｂ：我投宿在超級旅館。

▶▶ take sth. for granted 視⋯為理所當然

Ａ：Mike offered me a place to stay when I was in Nevada on business.

Ｂ：You shouldn't take his generosity for granted.

Ａ：當我去內華達州出差時，麥克提供我暫住的地方。
Ｂ：你不該視他的慷慨為理所當然。

▶▶ think over 仔細考慮

指對某事進行深度的思考與評量。

A : Will you make up your mind already? Are you going to come with us to Hawaii or not?

B : Just give me one more week to think it over.

A : 你已經下定決心了嗎？你到底要不要跟我們去夏威夷呢？

B : 再給我一週的時間來仔細考慮。

▶▶ **tip off** 向…洩露

A : How did he know where we'd be today?

B : Someone must have tipped him off.

A : 他如何知道我們今天會在哪裡呢？

B : 一定有人向他洩露。

PART

04 放輕鬆

▶▶ **a change of pace** 調劑一下心情

解說

指改變生活節奏，調劑一下心情。

A: You've been working at the computer all day. You need a change of pace. Would you like to see a movie with me tonight?

B: I would, but I have to finish this marketing plan tonight.

A: 你不要整天在電腦前工作，你需要調劑一下心情，你今晚想跟我去看電影嗎？

B: 我很想，但是我今晚必須完成這行銷計畫。

補充

看電影片語有 go to the movies，而 see a movie = watch a movie 是指看一場電影。

▶▶ **be on to** 識破

解說

指知道某事。

A : I think Nancy is on to us.

B : Nonsense, she has no idea we're planning a surprise birthday party for her.

A : 我想南茜識破我們。

B : 胡說，她不知道我們正打算為她舉辦一個驚喜生日派對。

▶▶ **be done with** 完全結束 / 放棄

解說

指未來不會再關心某事。

A : Do you want to join us at the bar tonight?

B : Actually, I think I'm done with drinking for a while. I need to start focusing on my career more, and not partying all the time.

PART

 A：你今晚要跟我們去酒吧嗎？

B：事實上，我想暫時戒酒，我需要開始更專心我的事業，而不是一直參加社交聚會。

補充

常用句型 It's done. = It's finished. 結束了。

▶▶ be hard to 很難

A：I heard the plot of movie is quite something.

B：But it is hard to follow.

 A：我聽說電影的情節很棒。

B：但是它很難懂。

補充

常用句型 Is that clear?（聽清楚了嗎？）

▶▶ be up to sth. 做好準備

A¹: We are all planning on going skydiving after winning the advertising campaign. Are you up to the challenge?

B²: Just as long as I am extremely drunk before I jump.

A¹: 在獲得廣告活動後,我們都打算去玩高空跳傘,你做好挑戰準備了嗎?

B²: 只要我喝很醉,我就敢跳。

▶▶ check off 核對

A¹: Have you checked off the list to make sure we have everything we need for the camping trip?

B²: Yes, we just need to stop at the store and get some beer.

A¹: 你有核對清單來確認我們去露營所需的每件東西都準備齊了嗎?

B²: 有啊,我們只需要在商店停一下,買些啤酒。

▶▶ come over 過來

A : So, are you still coming over after work?

B : Sorry, something has come up, and I won't be able to make it.

A : 所以，下班後，你還要過來嗎？
B : 抱歉，突然有事，所以我不能過去。

▶▶ come with 一起去

強調伴隨或同行。

A : We were thinking of going hiking this weekend. Would you like to come with us?

B : Sure, but I'll need to buy some hiking boots first.

A : 我們這週末想去爬山，你想要跟我們一起去嗎？
B : 當然可以，但是我得先買登山鞋。

補充

think of 考慮；come with = come along。

▶▶ **dead set on** 下定決心

解說

指堅定不移的立場或決定。

 I am dead set on going to Hawaii for the Christmas vacation.

B: What if no one wants to go with you?

A: 我下定決心要去夏威夷去度過我的聖誕節假期。

B: 萬一沒有人想跟你去怎麼辦呢？

▶▶ **get fit** 塑身

解說

就是要保持身材健美或健康。

A : I want to get fit, but I don't know where to begin.

B : Once you establish an exercise and diet program, before you know it, you'll start seeing results.

A : 我想要塑身，但是我不知如何下手。

B : 一旦你養成運動與飲食習慣，很快地，你會開始看到成果。

▶▶ **get rid of** 擺脫

指去除討厭的人或事。

A : I'm invited to a party on Sunday but I'm afraid that I won't be able to get rid of my cold by then.

B : Well, hope for the best.

A : 在星期日，我受邀參加宴會，但我擔心到時候我感冒還沒好。

B : 嗯，往最好處著想。

▶▶ go without saying 不用說

A : It'll be really hot and dry today.

B : It goes without saying that I should smear sun-screen and wear shades.

A : 今天天氣將會很炎熱乾燥。

B : 不用說，我應該塗上防曬霜和戴太陽眼鏡。

補充

tanning lotion ／ cream 助曬用品／油。

▶▶ good for a laugh 很有趣

A : Why do you always invite Peter to your par-ties? That guy gets on my nerves.

B : I know sometimes he can be annoying, but he's always good for a laugh.

A : 你為什麼總是邀請彼得來參加你的派對？那傢伙讓我不舒服。

B : 我知道他有時可能討人厭，但是他總是很有趣。

▶▶ in a word 總而言之

A : In a word, I think the party was a success.

B : Me, too. It couldn't have gone better.

A : 總而言之，我認為這派對辦得很成功。
B : 我也是這樣認為，這派對再成功不過了。

▶▶ in case 以防

A : Wear your shades in case the sun is too bright.

B : Thank you for reminding me. My eyes are sensitive to light.

A : 戴上太陽眼鏡，以防陽光太強。
B : 謝謝你提醒我，我的眼睛對光很敏感。

補充

常用句型為 Frequently asked questions in case of emergencies.（經常問問題來預防緊急事件。）

318

▶▶ knock off (work) 停止工作

解說

1. 有停止追求或做某事，如 I knocked off at five.（我五點停止工作。）
2. 減價 The company will knock off 500 dollars because you sign a contract.（因為你簽了約，公司會減價 500 美元。）
3.（低價）仿製品 Chinese knock off cell phone is a low quality product.（中國的山塞手機是低品質產品。）
4. 偷走 The stranger knocked off some jewelry.（這陌生人偷了一些珠寶。）

A: It's been a rough week at work. I could really use some rest and relaxation.

B: Why don't we knock off work and take a holiday?

A: 過去一週的工作是相當辛苦，我真的很需要放鬆一下。

B: 我們為什麼不停止工作去度假呢？

補充

rest and relaxation 放鬆一下，stop work 停止工作。

▶▶ **live up to** 遵守

解說

不辜負某事或滿足某人的要求。

 I wouldn't miss this farewell party for the world.

 I hope you will live up to your word.

 無論如何我也不會錯過歡送派對。

 我希望你會遵守你說的話。

▶▶ **make up to sb.** 補償某人

解說

此片語指對人的進行補償，若是對物進行補償，此片語必須為 make up for sth. 補償。

 I am sorry I missed your birthday party.

 I'll give you one chance to make it up to me.

 對不起，我錯過你的生日派對。

 我會給你一次機會來補償我。

▶▶ shake off 治好

用在疾病情境中，意思為「治好」。

A : There is a wonderful party at the shopping center this weekend.

B : If I can shake off the flu before this weekend, I will attend.

A : 這個週末在購物中心有一個很棒的舞會。

B : 如果我在週末前，能治好流感，我就會參加。

常用句型 I have the flu.（我得了流感。），其中 flu 前面須加定冠詞 the，不可加不定詞 a。

▶▶ stand sb. up 放某人鴿子

A : I can't believe you stood me up last night.

B : I'm sorry, but an emergency came up.

A : 我不敢相信你昨晚放我鴿子。

B : 對不起，有緊急事情發生。

PART

 興趣

▶▶ **as it is** 就保持原狀好了

A : Do you want a cigarette?

B : No, thanks. I have already too many bad habits as it is.

A : 你想抽根菸嗎？

B : 不，謝謝，我已經有很多壞習慣，就保持原狀好了。

▶▶ **at one time** 曾經

A : The song used to be my favorite.

B : I also liked it at one time, but not anymore.

：這首歌曾經是我最喜歡的歌。

B ：我曾經也喜歡它，但是現在不再是了。

▶▶ be crazy about 對…沉迷

(解)(說)

強調喜歡的意思。

A ：He's crazy about music.

B ：He is a musician, too.

A ：他沉迷音樂。

B ：他也是一位音樂家。

類似喜歡的句型有 He's hooked on music.（他沉迷於音樂。）／
He loves music.（他喜歡音樂。）／ He's a musicaholic.（他是一
位哈樂客。）

▶▶ for good 永遠

 : I want to quit smoking for good.

 : It is right to do so.

 : 我想要永遠戒掉抽菸。
 : 這樣做是對的。

補充

for good = forever

▶▶ I hear that... 我聽說

解說

I hear that + 子句 = Rumor has + 子句。

 : I hear that you play golf every weekend.

 : That's true.

 : 我聽說你每週末打高爾夫球。
 : 沒錯。

▶▶ **kick the habit 戒除習慣**

指戒掉壞習慣，如喝酒、吸毒或抽菸。

A: One of the hardest things to do is to quit smoking.

B: I agree. It took me seven years to kick the habit.

A: 戒菸是最難做的事情之一。

B: 我同意，我花了7年才戒掉這個習慣。

(補)(充)
1. kick sth. 放棄。
2. kick the habit = give up the habit，比如 No need to give up the habit of shopping online.（不需要戒除線上購物的習慣。）

▶▶ **look at 看**

注視某人或某物。

A : I like looking at these old pictures.

B : Me, too. I love looking at the way people used to be.

A : 我喜歡看這些老相片。

B : 我也是，我喜歡看人們過去的樣子。

---

used to 過去時常（而現在不再），I used to do everything by my-self.（我過去時常靠自己做每一件事。）；be used to 習慣於，I'm used to stay in the office overtime.（我習慣待在辦公室裡加班。）。

▶▶ **out of style** 過時了

指不時髦或過時。

A : You use the cellphone like it's going out of style.

B : Yes, it's out of style, but it's still the brand I love.

A ：你使用的手機好像快過時了。

B ：沒錯，它過時了，但是它仍是我喜歡的品牌。

(解)(說)

out of style = out of fashion；in style（流行）= in fashion。

 ▶▶ **put down 放下**

(解)(說)

直譯就是「放下」，而 put up 爲「舉起」或「抬高」的意思。

A ：Are you interested in the book?

B ：It's so good. I can't put it down.

A ：你對這本書有興趣嗎？

B ：它很棒，我不能放下它。（此句指「我愛不釋手」）。

▶▶ the thing 流行之物

A: I don't know what's "in" for spring.

B: Me, too. But I saw a lot of green shorts, so I guess that's the thing now.

A: 我不知道春天流行什麼。

B: 我也不知道,但是我看到許多綠色短褲,我猜那是現在時下流行之物。

補 充

這裡的 in 是指流行。

▶▶ What kind of 哪一種 / 什麼樣 / 什麼種類

A: What kind of job are you interested in?

B: I'm interested in a desk job.

A: 你對哪一種工作有興趣呢?

B: 我對文職工作有興趣。

類似的句型有 What kind of job do you like?（你喜歡哪一種工作？）／ What is your favorite type of job?（你最喜歡什麼類型的工作？）

國家圖書館出版品預行編目資料

口說職場生活英文片語會話／王仁癸著.--初
版.--臺北市：書泉，2015.06
　　面；　公分
　ISBN 978-986-451-005-4（平裝）
　1.英語　2.職場　3.會話　4.慣用語
805.188　　　　　　　　104007379

3AL2

口說職場生活英文片語會話

作　　　者 ─ 王仁癸(17.4)

發 行 人 ─ 楊榮川

總 編 輯 ─ 王翠華

主　　　編 ─ 朱曉蘋

責任編輯 ─ 吳雨潔

封面設計 ─ 吳佳臻

出 版 者 ─ 書泉出版社

地　　　址：106台北市大安區和平東路二段339號4樓

電　　　話：(02)2705-5066　　傳　　　真：(02)2706-6100

網　　　址：http://www.wunan.com.tw

電子郵件：shuchuan@shuchuan.com.tw

劃撥帳號：01303853

戶　　　名：書泉出版社

經 銷 商：朝日文化

進退貨地址：新北市中和區橋安街15巷1號7樓

TEL：(02)2249-7714　　　FAX：(02)2249-8715

法律顧問　林勝安律師事務所　林勝安律師

出版日期　2015年6月初版一刷

定　　　價　新臺幣400元